America

A Novel by
E. R. FRANK

SIMON PULSE

NEW YORK LONDON TORONTO SYDNEY SINGAPORE

First Simon Pulse edition August 2003
Copyright © 2002 by E. R. Frank

SIMON PULSE
An imprint of Simon & Schuster
Children's Publishing Division
1230 Avenue of the Americas
New York, NY 10020

Also available in an Atheneum Books for Young Readers hardcover edition.

Book design by Ann Bobco and Anne Scatto
The text of this book is set in Monotype Scotch.
Printed in the United States of America
1 2 3 4 5 6 7 8 9 10

The Library of Congress has cataloged the hardcover as follows:
Frank, E. R.
America / E. R. Frank.
p.   cm.
"A Richard Jackson book."
Summary: Teenage America, a part-black, part-white, part-anything
boy who has spent many years in institutions for disturbed,
antisocial behavior, tries to piece his life together.
ISBN 0-689-84729-7 (hc)
[1. Emotional problems—Fiction. 2. Racially mixed people—
Fiction.] I. Title.
PZ7.F84913 Am 2002
[Fic]—dc21   2001022984

ISBN 0-689-85772-1 (Simon Pulse pbk.)

America

Praise for *America*:

"Amazing grace from E. R. Frank."
—*New York Times Book Review*

★ "A piercing, unforgettable novel."
—*Booklist*, starred review

"This is a devastating portrayal of a teenager
who'd gotten lost in the system."
—*Book* magazine

★ "Moving."
—*School Library Journal*, starred review

"*America* is a jagged, beautiful story
of triumph, love, and understanding in
the face of neglect and depression."
—*Teenreads.com*

★ "Sublime."
—*Kirkus Reviews*, starred review

"A dramatic and heart-tugging story."
—*The Bulletin of the Center for Children's Books*

★ "Remarkable."
—*Publishers Weekly*, starred review

Also by E. R. Frank

Life Is Funny
Friction

*The author
gratefully acknowledges
and warmly thanks:*

Kathy Farrow,
Kerry Garfinkel,
Stacy Liss, and
Jessica Kalb Roland
for again taking on
the longest,
most tedious drafts.

Debbie Lefkovic-Abrams,
Laurie Lico-Albanese,
Julie Hess,
Amy Rosenblum,
Jim Rosenblum,
William Rosenblum, and
Ronni Saunders
for quick turnarounds
and valuable feedback.

Claire and Oren Cohen
for spirited support.

Lillian Frank
for being a terrific grandma.

Charlotte Sheedy
for knowing which way to go
and how to get there.

Richard Jackson
for so gracefully
living up to the legend.

For stephen

Now

You have to watch what you say here because everything you say means something and somebody's always telling you what you mean.

"Step off," I tell this nurse when she tries to get me to eat.

"You mean, thank you for caring," she says. "You're welcome."

"I need a lighter," I tell her, and she goes, "You mean you want a lighter. Dream on, sweetheart."

So I take their medicine and walk around in socks the way they make you, and stay real quiet.

— • • —

"Hello, America," he goes. "I'm Dr. B." He holds out his hand, but I play like I don't even see it. "I'll be your therapist while you're here at Ridgeway." He drops his arm like it's no big thing and dumps his skinny butt in a chair behind his desk. "You can sit anywhere." He doesn't have any tennis balls or messed-up eyeglasses or an attitude like those other ones back at Applegate. He's just regular. I stay standing. "We'll meet at this time for forty-five minutes every Tuesday and Thursday." I keep my back right up on the door. He's all calm, like it's cool with him. "Our sessions will be confidential. Are you familiar with the rules of confidentiality?" I don't bother answering. "Confidentiality means what's said in this room stays in this room." He stops a second, looking at me, close. "Except for three things." Looking at me straight up. "If you tell me that someone is harming you, if you express the intent to harm yourself, or do so, or if you express the intent to harm anyone else, or do so. Those three things don't stay private between us."

"That's it?" I go.

"'That's it,' what?" he goes. Not in my face. Just normal.

"That's all you've got, if I say I'm going to off myself?"

"Is that what you're planning?"

"Huh?"

"Are you planning to kill yourself?"

"That's not what I asked."

"I know that's not what you asked." He's leaning forward on his elbows, like he's interested, like he for real even cares.

"It's no big secret, doc," I go. "How the hell do you think I got here?"

They try to make me do group.

"Who wants to share with America what the purpose of this group is?" the lady goes.

Nobody bothers, so she picks on some kid all bent over with his arms crossed looking like he's got nails twisting up his stomach. "Don?" the lady goes, and he squeaks his chair and crosses his arms the other way.

"Supposed to talk or something," this Don goes. I'm out of here.

"Please sit down, America," the lady tells me. I head for the door. "America, you are required to participate in group," the lady goes. I keep walking. "Privileges," I hear her yelling.

Points, tickets, privileges. You do this, they give you that many. You get that many, they let you out. Let you out where? Some other sorry-ass place. I don't need this.

 ● ● ●

I'm not stupid. I know it's going to get real tiring standing by his door for near to an hour. So I sit this time.

"I guess you're not in the mood to talk," Dr. B. goes, after a lot of minutes. I lean my head over the back of the chair and stare up at the ceiling. "I guess you're not much in the mood to be here, either," Dr. B. says, all calm.

"You're some genius," I go.

 ● ● ●

A week. Maybe two. I don't know, and I don't care. I'm just slamming my pillow on the floor every night. Sleeping on my back, flat out, with my arms straight down my sides. Like I'm in a coffin.

＊ ＊ ＊

"It's hard to know how to begin."

"What's that supposed to mean?"

His ceiling is white stripes and a round light in the middle.

"Just what it says," he goes. "Sometimes, it's hard for people to begin their sessions."

"Ah, man." My neck aches, bad, but I keep my head hanging over the back of my chair anyway.

"You seem annoyed."

"Yeah, I'm annoyed. Who wouldn't be?"

"Maybe that's part of why it's hard to start each session."

"Maybe you're repeating yourself."

"Maybe you're so annoyed to start with, it makes you not want to talk."

"Whatever."

"What would it be like if you did talk?"

"I talk, man."

"Not so much."

"So?"

"I'm curious about what keeps you from talking."

"Well, you're going to have to live with curious a long time, doc."

＊ ＊ ＊

You get in line, and you slide your tray, and they hand over your baby carrots and your chicken and your roll, and you sit at some table with a million other dudes, and you eat, and it tastes like your own tongue, and you wish you could just choke to death once and forever right here, right in the middle of nothing.

— • —

"Some people believe that depression is anger turned toward the self," Dr. B. says.

He might not have attitude like those other ones back at Applegate, but he's got the same old pile of stupid games. Connect Four and checkers. Chess and Monopoly and all that. I grab his Uno cards and knuckle-shuffle them.

"It's just something to know," Dr. B. says. "Because usually people who try to kill themselves are depressed, and often they're depressed because they're angry."

I shuffle again and then slap the stack down on his desk.

"People who are able to somehow acknowledge their anger often become less depressed."

"Cut the deck," I go, because he's giving me a headache with all that.

— • —

I try not to think about it in the rec room. I watch those guys play Ping-Pong, and I try not to think. About that anger mess. About depressed. Only every time I remember that cement rectangle with a footprint in one corner, I watch Mrs. Harper sending me away, and whenever I see Clark Poignant, it's when he's got tubes running all into the backs of his hands, and if I try to picture Liza, I just hear how she said she'd hate me if I ever killed myself, and anytime Brooklyn's face pops up in my head, I see him stealing those green Magic Markers. And every time I think about baseball, I see Browning.

I watch that Ping-Pong , and I try not to think.

•━•━•

"What would it be like?" Dr. B. goes.

"Huh?"

"Being dead."

"Huh?"

"You're interested in being dead. I'm interested in what you think being dead would be like."

"You're the doctor, man. You tell me."

"I don't know. Different people imagine different things. I'm wondering what you imagine."

Empty. Quiet. Nobody's good. Nobody's bad. Nobody's nobody. You don't think. You don't remember. You don't be. Nothing hurts.

"Step off," I tell him.

"Hmm," he goes.

•━•━•

CONTRACT FOR SAFETY

I, America, agree that if I feel I might harm myself, I will immediately follow the plan below:

1) Notify on-duty nurse of my feelings.
2) Write down the date and time.
3) Write down the name of each feeling I'm experiencing, followed by the thoughts and/or events which preceded it.

4) Notify and discuss all of the above with Dr. B. immediately upon our next scheduled session.

In addition, I give my promise that I will not try to harm or kill myself, should I experience the wish to do so.

It's one of the most messed-up things I ever heard in my whole stupid life. If you feel so bad you want to die, why would you even care what kind of lame-ass promises you make?

I'm not signing shit.

— • • •

"Some kids don't want to feel better," Dr. B. says. So what. "Because it's too frightening," he goes, and then he stops. I'm resting my head over the back of this chair and staring up at his ceiling. "Think about it a second."

"I don't like to think." I hang my head way far back and see his bookshelves upside down behind me. Instead of books, they've got some kind of little statues lined up. Dollhouse people, or something.

We're quiet for a real long time, but then he goes, "I'm guessing you're used to feeling mad and bad."

"So?" I go.

"Feeling better would be something you don't know."

"You got that right," I tell him.

"A lot of people are scared of what they don't know. So they hold on to mad and bad."

I'm not even going to play like I know what all he's saying. So I stay quiet.

⟶ • • •

My pills used to be green. Wheatgrass, Mrs. Harper would say. Then blue. Now yellow. They're all the same shape. Stretched-out ovals. The nurse brings me one every morning and watches me swallow it. I don't care. Some people take all different ones. A mess of colors, and all these shapes. They try to hold their pill under their tongue, or sick it up after the nurse leaves. It's likely a million pills these nurses have to keep all stocked up here. Somebody's making a straight-up fortune.

⟶ • • •

"How many weeks have I been here?" I go to the group lady.

"Excuse me?"

"I didn't know that kid could talk," some scrub goes.

"How long have I been here?"

"About three weeks," the group lady says. "Is that something you'd like to speak about?"

I shrug and stare at this crack on the wall, this crack that does the shape of a big-ass crumpled square. It looks like a TV after someone smashed up all the corners. I watch it for the whole rest of the time, so I don't know how I get to noticing it, but all of them that used to be in this group are gone except me. It's new guys now, and I'm the only old one.

⟶ • • •

"All right," Dr. B. goes, after I won't play Uno anymore, and I won't play anything else, and I still won't talk, either. "Where would you like to be five years from now?"

"Nowhere," I tell him.

• • •

The thing is, Mrs. Harper might be alive. She might be in some bed somewhere, in some nursing home, just hoping for someone to come see her.

Or she could be hanging out with Clark Poignant up there in Heaven. Dead.

• • •

This one kid screams at night. If Liza or Brooklyn were here, either one, they'd find out quick right where he's at and tell him to shut the hell up. This kid's in some other hall or wing or someplace. The screaming's not real loud, because must be he's far away, but it's bad. It's the kind that makes you picture a movie scene with some crazy-looking dude, wrapped in sheets, all sweaty and bug-eyed. Like something real, real deep went down with him he's likely never going to get out of his head.

I'm betting he's real pissed they're keeping him alive.

• • •

I could ask, but I'm too tired. So I listen instead. I listen to the nurses chitchatting, and I listen to the other guys telling all their private business and everybody else's, and I listen to Dr. B. even when he thinks I'm not. You figure out a real lot when you're just quiet and you listen.

Here's what I figure out. This place, Ridgeway, has just about everything. It's got buildings for girls and buildings for boys and buildings for both. It's got buildings for real serious, like me, where you live, and for people who sleep somewhere else but come in here for the day. It's got a building for if you're here because a judge made you, and it's got a building for if you're all used up from drugs. The street kind, not their kind.

Me. I was in emergency first, right after I tried to off myself back at Applegate. Emergency drugged me up intense for a while, and then they didn't drug me up as much, and then emergency kicked my butt out and put me here. Most people stay about a month, maybe two, and then go somewhere else. They go home for good, or else to sleep at night and then back to Ridgeway or some other place for day treatment. Or they skip home and land right in long-term residential. That's what Applegate was, long-term residential treatment. I wasn't supposed to get sent there in the first place. I should have gone to some group home. Some foster care group home, only the system screwed up. Stupid thing is, right now I would go back to Applegate, only they just got this new rule of not letting kids in older than thirteen, and the other long-term residential eighteen miles away is full, and the rest are out of my district, so I'm not allowed in, and there's no beds left in any group homes, and the only places left besides here is jail, which is where I know I ought to be. Or else a state hospital, but you only get sent to a state hospital if you're so far gone, you're pulling out your eyeballs thinking they're grapes, or some damn thing.

So I'm here.

* * *

"You only let people out after they spill their guts, right?"

"What do you mean?"

"I'm saying, you only let people leave this place if they're all talking every minute in their sessions, right?"

"Something's given you that idea?"

"Hell yeah, man. I see how it is. It's those guys who talk that get to leave. Like that Don guy from group. He used to never say boo, then all of a sudden you can't shut him up. He's talking every second, and bang. He's out of here."

"I see."

"Well, I'm not telling you jack."

"You think if you start sharing your thoughts and feelings with me, you'll leave here more quickly?"

"I don't think. I know."

"So you've decided not to talk."

"Yup."

"So you don't want to leave here."

"I didn't say that."

"So you do want to leave here," he goes.

"So, nothing, man."

"Maybe you have mixed feelings about it. Maybe sometimes you want to be here and other times you don't."

"Can you just be quiet a second?"

"Or, maybe, sometimes right at the same time you want to be here and also you don't."

"I asked you to shut up. You're making me dizzy."

—•—•—•—

We play checkers. You don't have to think. You don't have to talk. Say things that might make you remember, might make them send you away when you've got no place to go. No house, because you burned it right down to the ground, no shopping mall to hide out in, or bushes in a park. No couch up for grabs in some dude's crib. No nothing.

—•—•—•—

I'm listening to that kid screaming from whichever wing they've got him in, and I wish I had my shoelaces. You can see good enough in the middle of the night here because they keep the hall lights on, and I could hypnotize my sorry self the way they do in those cartoons where some hanging watch going back and forth makes a dude black out even though the guy's awake and all. I could tie something heavy to the end of a shoelace and swing it back and forth in front of my face and stare and stare, keeping my head real still, and letting my eyes go all side to side, and make myself get all spaced out. Only problem is these Ridgeway nurses, man. They took my shoelaces, and damn if I can find anything else to use.

—•—•—•—

"If you're so interested in my business, why don't you just read my file?"

"Your file."

"I know you've got a file on me, doc. Don't even try to play like you don't."

"I'm not trying anything," he goes.

"So what are you bothering me for?" I go. "You lazy or something? Just read the file."

"Actually, I've read it."

"Then why do you need to talk to me?"

"Why do you think I might need to talk to you?"

"I don't know, man."

"I'm aware that you don't know. I'm just wondering what you think."

"I don't like to think."

"Yes. You've said that before."

"Okay. What do I think? I think it's your job."

"What does that mean?"

"What do you mean, 'What does that mean?' It's your job. It's a job."

"Hmm." Sometimes, he's just stupid.

"So what's in my file, anyway?"

"What do you imagine is in the file?"

"Are you for real?"

"Yes. What do you imagine?"

"I don't go around imagining."

‑ ‑ ‑

That file probably says how I was in special ed. How I cursed at teachers and stole lighters and made Mrs. Harper sick. It probably says something like, *America is a boy who is a lot of trouble. America is a boy who is crazy. America might be a murderer. Be real careful of America.* That's probably what it says. That's how those files go.

I must be walking my ass from the bed to the cafeteria to the rec room to his office, but I don't know. I just end up wherever I am. I can't hardly remember how I even got here.

⸻ • ⸻ • •

"How's it laid out?" I go.

"What do you mean?"

"Damn, Dr. B. Am I going to have to explain every last little thing?"

"Maybe," he goes.

"How's the order of it? Is it all one paper, like somebody telling some story about me, or is it all blanks and squares and like that?"

"You're asking me how your file is organized?"

"That's what I'm asking."

"Well, how are you picturing it?"

"Would you stop with that, man? I swear to God."

"Stop with what?"

"With that picturing shit. I'm not stupid. I know picturing's the same as imagining."

"Hmm."

"So just answer my question."

"All right," he goes. "Your file has a sort of story about you as well as blanks and squares."

"How's the story set up?"

"There's a section about your medical history. Another section about your school history. There's a section about your people and growing-up history. And other sections."

"How are you supposed to know if they got all

those sections right about me, if I don't even get to check it out my own self?"

"You want to be sure what I read about you is accurate."

"That's what I'm saying."

"One way I could know that is to have you tell me about your own self, your own self."

"Nice try, doc."

"I'm not trying anything, America."

— • • •

I'm flat straight without any pillow on my coffin bed. Here's what I imagine. The growing-up section starts with me getting born. It goes like this: *America got born to a crack addict who didn't want him. Two days after that, America got with a rich white family, only they didn't want him after he started turning his color. So in a couple of months quick, America got taken by the rich white family's nanny.*

I'm flat straight without any pillow on my coffin bed and I decide imagining is right up there with thinking. Don't like either one.

— • • •

"You're going to blackmail me, right?"

"What do you mean?"

"You're going to make me tell you all my private business before you let me see the file."

"Really."

"What else? You're doing your job the way they tell you. Trying real hard to get me to give it up. So now you're all, 'America, you tell me your business, and I'll show you the file.'"

"Hmm."

"I'm not telling you shit."

◆ ◆ ◆

"You dropped your pillow." I didn't used to see these other beds right next to mine. "Hey," this new kid's going. "I think you dropped your pillow." Must have been weeks before I even got to noticing this room, much less any of these other guys in here with me. Thing is, they change over so many times, I never know who all is going to be in the next bed.

"Here," this new dude goes. He picks up my stupid pillow and drops it on my legs.

◆ ◆ ◆

America is a boy who's been a lot of places. I bet that's what that file says somewhere. *America is a boy who gets lost easy and is not worth the trouble of finding.*

◆ ◆ ◆

He's all leaning forward on his elbows. "There's an opening at a group home." That's how it works. You stay awhile one place, and then you go. "Medicaid's been clear with us that stays on this unit are to be short-term only. You've been here over six weeks. A time frame Medicaid does not consider to be short-term."

"Medicaid's same as the state, right?"

"I'm not sure what you mean."

"You know exactly what I mean. It's all the same. Medicaid. The state. They're all the same damn thing."

"America, if you're still unable to sign the safety contract. I'm not sure the group home will take you, regardless of Medicaid's requirements."

16

"I guess you and Medicaid have a problem, then, doc."

"So you're still thinking of killing yourself?"

"I don't think, man. I keep telling you."

— ⋆ — ⋆ — ⋆ —

America's nanny's name was Mrs. Harper. Mrs. Harper was real good to America. Also Mrs. Harper's half-brother, whose name was Browning, was real good to America. Also, Mrs. Harper's man friend, Clark Poignant, was real real good to America. But then, America turned out to be bad and made people sick, so Mrs. Harper and the state sent America back to his mother. But then America's mother had better things to do and left America with his two older brothers. Lyle was the oldest one, but Brooklyn was the baddest, so Brooklyn was in charge. That's probably in there, too. Stupid-ass files.

— ⋆ — ⋆ — ⋆ —

I watch those guys play Ping-Pong, and I try not to think. Trouble is, the more you try not to think, the more you end up thinking.

This is what I think. You can know who you're mad at but still know you're bad and ought to be dead. Partly because just knowing who you're mad at doesn't make you any less bad and partly because if you do get better the way they want, then the feelings are going to come crashing down on you like some kind of goddamn avalanche.

— ⋆ — ⋆ — ⋆ —

"If you let me read my file, I'll sign your stupid safety contract, and you can get rid of me to that group home," I go.

"First of all, the safety contract doesn't work that way."

"What way?"

"The safety contract is not some sort of trading tool. It stands on its own. And second, what makes you believe I'm trying to get rid of you?"

"Because that's what you're doing, man."

• • •

I sleep in that room with all the dudes who show up and leave again. Some kid with an earring who used to be in cottage two back at Applegate shows up four beds over for a week and then disappears. I don't care. I stand in that cafeteria line and eat their nastiness. I sit in group and don't listen and watch Ping-Pong in the rec room. That's all I do, besides try not to think.

• • •

He won't show me the file, and I won't sign the contract, and he won't sign for me to leave, and some other kid gets my spot in the group home.

"Looks like we're stuck with each other, doc," I go.

"Stuck," he goes.

"S-T-U-C-K. Stuck," I go. "Rhymes with fuck."

"Hmm."

"Should have let me read the file, man."

"What is it about the file that feels so important, America?"

"Can you shut up with your stupid questions? Just bring it out, already."

"I'm sorry, but I can't do that right now."

"Why not?"

"Partly because I'm not comfortable showing it until we've talked further about what reading it might be like for you."

"Huh?"

"Reading your file could bring up feelings, America. It's a complicated thing to read what other people write about you. I think it might feel too complicated for you to handle right now."

Those files probably only have the bad. *America is a thief and a wrecker of property. America did not learn to read right until he was almost ten years old. America is a runaway.* They only have all the messed-up stuff. They don't have the smaller things. The parts that matter.

"What is it about the file that feels so important to you, America?"

A red ball lollipop. The UPS man who delivers the angels and picks them up again gives it to me. When I get to the fizz in the middle, Mrs. Harper smiles at my face and touches my chin and says, "Real meaning is in the smaller things."

"It's mine, man."

That smell of mint leaves on Mrs. Harper's hands, same as the Chap Stick she makes me smear on in the winter. A rusty streak in Clark Poignant's silver hair. The way he always brings Mrs. Harper white tulips cut straight from his garden and teaches me to shake hands, real firm and solid. The sweet smell of Browning's brown cigarettes.

"It's yours?" Dr. B. goes.

"That's right, man. My business is mine. I own that shit."

I hide under the paint table, and Mrs. Harper goes, "Where is America?" And I pop up, and she goes, "There he is!" And I scream because it's real good to get found. And she stands up from her stool and puts down her fresh-painted blue-and-gold angel real gentle and goes, "I see you, Mister. I see you over there." And I scream because it's real good to be seen. And she pulls off her smock and goes, "I'm going to get you, America! I'm going to get you!" And I'm banging out the screen door running real hard and laughing real hard, and she's running right after me and laughing, too, and she's going to snatch me up any minute and hold me real close and tickle, and I run harder, and then she catches me, and she's going, "I got you! I got you!" and she's got me right down between her warm self and the scratchy grass, and she's wiggling her fingers up under my arms, and we're laughing like crazy, and I'm screaming my head off.

"My not letting you read your business makes you feel I'm taking away something that's yours," Dr. B. goes.

"Huh?"

I help Mrs. Harper screw the paint caps on and soak the brushes, and those angels stand and fly and kneel and sit on our built-in bookshelves waiting to dry off, get repacked, and sent back to the people who pay us for them. They cover every wall of Mrs. Harper's workroom, the great big mess of them protecting the whole house, like a real pretty army.

"Maybe you could just tell me more about your business being yours," Dr. B. says.

"I told you, doc. I'm not telling you anything."

— • • • —

I lie flat out straight in my coffin bed, and it's getting on my nerves. How Dr. B. gets things going in my head, making me see things I don't hardly care to see. That's the problem with talking to people. All that talking makes you get cracks in your brain, and then all these flashes start leaking right on through.

— • • • —

"You seem extra quiet today." I've got my neck fixed on the back of my chair and my eyes all open on that round light.

"I'm always quiet. Nothing extra about it." I lean my head back more and check out those sand people on that bookshelf behind me, all upside down. They're gray and little, the size of my fingers.

"Maybe what I mean is that I'm noticing you're not interested in playing any games today and you haven't looked at me at all."

"Whatever." They've got guns and drums and all that. Soldiers. A bunch of soldiers.

"Maybe something's happened that's brought up some feelings."

"Nothing's happened, man. I eat. I sleep. I piss. I go to group. I come here. Time up yet?"

"Almost. Those are things that happen for you on the outside. Maybe something else has happened with you on the inside that's brought up some feelings."

I'm sitting in a booster seat in the middle of Clark Poignant and Mrs. Harper and Browning, and it's real calm. I'm filling in the coloring book page with crayons the waitress gave me.

"Look," Mrs. Harper goes. "It's America." She points her finger with the round, black ring to my page.

Clark Poignant says, "That's a map of where we live."

"That's New York," Mrs. Harper says. "That's in America. We live in New York in America."

"I'm America," I tell them.

"Yup," Browning goes, hanging his arm over my shoulder. "You're America."

"America is the place where we live, and it's also your name," Mrs. Harper says.

"I'm in America," I say. "And America is me." I like saying that. I like the sound of it and the beat of it and the way it makes Mrs. Harper and Clark Poignant and Browning smile. So I say it again. "I'm in America, and America is me."

"We're done now, if you want to leave." I sit up.

"Huh?"

"I said," Dr. B. goes, "we're done for today."

◆ ◆ ◆

You try not to think. You try not to imagine, but then those cracks pop up, and these flashes squeeze right through. At first, some of it's not too bad, and you get stupid, maybe even wanting a little more, but then you pull yourself together, knowing what all is likely going to ooze out if you're not careful. So you try to patch up this one crack real quick, but then some other one pops up faster than you can spit, and then you've got to rush your ass around trying to keep things shut tight. That's the problem with being in one place too long. You're at somewhere too long, and your brain gets weak. It's enough to drive a person straight out of his own mind.

—●—●—●—

"So how long am I staying here, anyway, doc?" I go.

"How long do you want to stay here?"

"Who says I want to stay here?"

"I'm just remembering the time you mentioned you weren't planning to talk much because you believed talking meant you would leave soon."

"So?"

"So I took that to mean that a part of you would like to stay here."

"Well, I don't know what all you're talking about now, man."

"Hmm."

"Anyway, I don't stay places long."

"What's long?"

"What do you mean, 'What's long?'"

"I mean, how long is long. A week? A year?"

Clark Poignant's in his bed, even though it's light outside, and he has his own nurse, even though his house isn't a hospital.

"Saturday will go by quicker than you think," he tells me. "You'll be back home before you know it. And then Monday you'll start kindergarten." He raises his

arm to touch my shoulder, the way he always does, and I'm scared the tube in the back of his hand will slide out, making him bleed.

"He's just confused," Mrs. Harper says when I hide behind her. A little rip in her voice makes me look up at her face and then grab her finger with the black, round ring on it. I rub the top of the ring, and she lets me, and it's smooth and feels good.

"Kindergarten," Clark Poignant says. "Can you believe it?"

"An unsupervised visit," Mrs. Harper says back, with that rip again. "That's what I can't believe."

"Does he know how to call us?" Clark Poignant asks Mrs. Harper, and she says, "He's got everybody's number memorized," and then I make them smile by saying all the numbers. It's a lot to remember, but Mrs. Harper said a boy my age could do it, and I did. "Tell Clark about collect," Mrs. Harper says, so I do, and he says when I get home to call him collect for practice.

Back at Mrs. Harper's, on the upstairs phone, I push zero, just like she showed me, and I give out Clark Poignant's number, and the operator goes, "Who can I say is calling?"

"America," I say, and Mrs. Harper smiles at me from her rocking chair. I hold the phone out to her for a second, but Mrs. Harper waves it back at me, and then Clark Poignant's voice is on the line, and he's saying, "Good job. Good job." I like the way his voice is real still and buzzes fast, like the way a bee's body is real *still and buzzes fast around a flower, both at the same time.*

"Long is long, man. Long is whenever they feel like deciding," I go.

"Who's 'they,' America?"

"The state," I tell Dr. B. "Medicaid."

"The state and Medicaid?" Dr. B. goes.

"Now you're getting on my nerves, man."

Before my visit to my mother, Mrs. Harper's going to paint something special with all her angels.

"Can you sit still for half a second?" she goes. I don't figure I can, but if I say no, she'll think I'm being mouthy.

"Do I have to go?" I say to Mrs. Harper.

"You do," she says. "But it's only for Saturday, America. And then you'll come right home, and Monday after that, you'll start your kindergarten."

"If I act extra good, do I have to go?" I ask her.

"Has nothing to do with how you act," she says. "I keep telling you."

"What if she wants to abduct me?" I say.

"Adopt you. Not abduct you," Mrs. Harper says. "She doesn't have to adopt you. You're already hers. She's your mother. I'm the one trying to adopt you."

"What about the papers?" I ask her.

"What do you know about papers?" Mrs. Harper says, and I'm scared she's going to look at me hard and turn her back, the way she does when I've made her mad, but she just pats her paintbrush over angel wings.

"Browning said she could write her name on a paper

and then the state would let her keep the paper and let
you keep me and I wouldn't have to visit her."

"She doesn't want to write her name," Mrs. Harper
says.

"How come?" I ask.

Mrs. Harper looks real hard at her wet wings and
then throws the angel down. It breaks into pieces. She
never broke one before, ever, and especially not on
purpose. "I don't know," she tells me. "I really don't
know."

"I'm getting on your nerves," Dr. B. goes.

"Can you stop repeating every other thing I say?"
I go. "Damn."

"Unfortunately it's a bad habit of mine, but I'll
try to stop."

"Why don't you just try to be quiet?"

"You're pretty aggravated right now."

"I'm not aggravated. I'm pissed."

Browning's gin root beer smells nasty. His bag of
Tootsie Rolls is stuffed in my back pocket. It's heavy,
like it might just take my pants right down.

"Don't you have yourself together yet?" Mrs. Harper
goes after dinner, and I wonder which part of him fell
off: his head, or his arms, or his legs. Then I wonder
if he has wings, so I go to check, but before I can see,
Mrs. Harper sends us outside. "If I've told you once,
I've told you a million times," she goes to Browning.
"I'm not having liquor in this house." So now Brown-
ing holds his gin root beer in one hand and throws me
the Wiffle ball with the other.

"Now listen," Browning says, tossing me an easy one. "We're buddies, right?"

"Yeah," I say, hitting it straight to his chest. He drops his root-beer can and claps both hands around the ball quick, the way I catch fireflies.

"So listen to me careful," Browning says. "More careful than you ever listened before. Okay?"

"Yeah," I say, waiting for the next pitch.

"Because what I'm about to say is real different from what Mrs. Harper and Clark have been telling you. Okay?"

"Okay," I say. "Pitch it." He pitches it. I hit a pop fly. He catches it behind his back. Then he sits on his butt in the grass and waves his hand at me to come get next to him. I do, and our faces are real close. His breath smells. He talks real low.

"What you have to do is, when you get to your mother's tomorrow, as soon as you get there, as much as you can, you be bad."

"Be bad?" I back up from his breath.

"That's what I'm trying to say." He pulls a brown cigarette from behind his ear and sets it between his lips without lighting it. "Don't listen to anything your mother tells you. Do as many bad things as you know how. Act like a real bad kid. Okay?" His cigarette moves up and down in time with what he's saying.

"I don't want to."

"If you act bad," he says, "that mother of yours will make sure to send you home right back here to Mrs. Harper before your day is even up, and she *won't ever want you to visit again, much less want to keep you."*

"But Mrs. Harper will be mad." *If I do it like he says, she'll end up looking at me hard and turning her back.* "Mrs. Harper will get extra mad."

"Nope," he tells me. "She won't be mad as long as she gets you home for good."

"But—"

"I've told you what to do," Browning says, messing with a dandelion. He knows how to tie a knot in it and then snap the stem so the flower part flies off. "If you want your mother to leave us all be." He shrugs at me and flicks the dandelion top. The flower hits my eye. "It's up to you."

"What's pissed you off?" Dr. B. goes.

"You."

"What is it that I've done?"

"Step off."

"Please sit down, America."

"I'm out of here."

"We have five minutes left, America."

"Fuck your five minutes."

"I'll see you Thursday then."

"Oh, yeah? Fuck Thursday."

◦ ◦ ◦

I fuck Thursday. I keep my ass in the rec room watching Ping-Pong. I watch that ball popping all back and forth. I watch it careful, concentrating real hard, and doing that shit helps keep those cracks in my brain sealed up tight. It works so good,

I almost don't even notice Dr. B. hanging out in the doorway awhile, looking at me.

● ● ●

"Something kept you from coming to our session Thursday."

"Whatever."

"I looked for you." *America gets lost easy.* "I found you in the rec room." *And is not worth the trouble of finding.* "I was interested in what it was that took you to the rec room instead of to our session." He's got a regular deck of cards in his stupid pile of games.

"War," I go.

"Something happened that kept you from our session, America."

"You know the rules?" I'm knuckle-shuffling.

"You don't want to discuss what happened."

"I asked if you know the rules, man."

"I'm not sure if I know your rules." I slap down the deck. He cuts it.

"Two of spades beats everything, including aces. Aces beat everything but the two of spades. Count your cards."

"Twenty-five," Dr. B. goes.

"Twenty-seven," I go. "Here. Pick one." He picks. "Now we're even."

"All right."

"So throw down, man." We throw down. "See that?" I say. "We got war already."

"War."

"Well, let's go then, doc," I say. "I De Clare War."

Then

It's Saturday afternoon, and my mother was here earlier, but then she left on an errand. I'm waiting by the window so I can see her coming back, but I'm so high up, everybody down there on the street looks all the same. Like fleas. And the cars look like toys. But if I stay by the window, Brooklyn and Lyle won't bother me. They took the rest of my Tootsie Rolls already, and Brooklyn punched my ear, but then when I got by the window, they changed the channel on the TV and started ignoring me.

I get to thinking about yesterday morning and how I'd found Mrs. Harper in her workroom, the walls all filled up with finished angels. About how those angels were perfect. All the same, a zillion same, all like me. It made me scream my hide-and-seek scream, my tag-and-tickle, you-can't-catch-me scream. Those angels had brown hair that wasn't real straight and not too curly, and yellow flecks inside green eyes with a flat shape on the outsides, and reddish-brown skin and wings, and puffy mouths and skinny noses. I screamed good and loud, and I must have scared Mrs. Harper real bad because when she lifted her head from the table, it looked like maybe she was a little bit crying.

— • • —

"I'm supposed to go home now," I go.

"Where that?" Brooklyn goes.

"Two forty-two Willow Road, Nyack, New York," I go. Then I say all my numbers.

"Never heard of no Nyack," Brooklyn goes. "You in New York City now, bro."

"Yup," Lyle goes.

"He not going nowhere," Brooklyn goes to Lyle.

"Where's the phone?" I go.

"Where the phone?" Lyle goes to Brooklyn.

"Under the sink," Brooklyn goes. I leave the window and look under the kitchen sink, but it's just cockroaches under there. "The bathroom sink," Brooklyn goes, but there's just more cockroaches and a phone without any cords anywhere for plugging in.

"Do your neighbors have a phone?" I go.

"You bother the neighbors, Mama going to beat your ass," Lyle goes.

— • • —

Our mother isn't home yet from her errand, and it's real dark outside the window. Brooklyn says I get to share the sofa bed with Lyle. But Lyle says he's saving it for Kyle, and makes me sleep on the floor. The floor is the same kind of floor as Mrs. Harper's kitchen. It's gray and black squares. It's the floor of the whole apartment. It's hard and cold. Lyle won't let me have Kyle's share of the blankets or pillows. Brooklyn says Kyle isn't even alive. He says Kyle's dead, but Lyle's crazy and pretends Kyle is just away visiting somewhere, but Brooklyn doesn't make Lyle share the bed.

I'm real sore all over, plus I'm cold, but when the light starts outside, I stand up by the window again to wait for my mother or Mrs. Harper to come get me. I don't see them, either one, down there in the middle of all those fleas, though, and then Brooklyn and Lyle get up and eat cereal without any milk. After that I think I see the lady who took me on the bus from Mrs. Harper's house to a taxi to an office where my mother got me. I think I see that lady for a minute, but they all look too much the same down there, and it's not her.

—•—•—•—

Brooklyn and Lyle go out. They leave me alone in the apartment, and I look for a phone that works somewhere, but I can't find one.

—•—•—•—

When they get back, it's close to nighttime again, and I'm real hungry, and I get to crying. I'm supposed to start kindergarten tomorrow.

"Shut up," Brooklyn goes. I get to crying harder. "Shut up, or I'll throw your ass out the window," he tells me. But then Lyle walks right up and punches my eye, and I shut up, and Brooklyn forgets about throwing me out the window.

Our mother hasn't gotten back yet, and Mrs. Harper doesn't come get me, and Clark Poignant can't because he's too sick in his bed, and Browning doesn't come, either, and there's no phones, and I don't start kindergarten. When I cry, Brooklyn and Lyle, one or the other, hit me, and I spend a real lot of hours looking out the window, waiting hard.

Brooklyn is the baddest seven-year-old you ever knew. Brooklyn smokes regular white cigarettes and watches the naked channel and **MTV** and the cartoon channel. Brooklyn cooks toast for us and ravioli out of a can and peanut-butter-and-jelly sandwiches. Brooklyn knows how to clear the toilet so it will flush again, and he knows every bad word they ever invented, even some in Spanish. Also, Brooklyn knows how to pee out the window into the air shaft and how to steal from the stores downstairs and from the tables on the street. Brooklyn is very, very bad and knows everything.

He tells me not to leave out the apartment until after ravioli because I'm supposed to be in school, and if our mama finds out anybody else finds out we're not doing school, she'll beat our ass the minute she gets back from her errand. Brooklyn likes Slim Jims, which he steals from downstairs, and he likes things that are green. He uses a Magic Marker to color all of his underwear green. Brooklyn likes my eyes because they're green, but they make him mad, too. When Brooklyn gets mad at me, he knocks me down. Sometimes I just stay on the gray and black floor when he's around so I'm down already and don't have to get knocked. Brooklyn isn't mad when he needs someone to play I Declare War or jacks. Brooklyn stole the cards, and I stole the jacks from a table outside. I thought maybe I'd get to go home then because stealing is bad, but nobody saw.

◆ ◆ ◆

"When does our mother get back?" I say to Lyle.

"She not your mama," he goes.

"She is, too," I go.

Brooklyn's shuffling the deck, one-handed. We're getting ready to play three-way War.

"When does she get back?" I ask Brooklyn. He slams the deck down. Lyle cuts it.

"How does I know?" Brooklyn goes. "She on a errand." He deals out the cards.

"But when is she coming back?"

"She coming back," Brooklyn goes.

"Yeah, but when?"

"Shut up."

◆ ◆ ◆

Brooklyn lets us go out on Saturdays and Sundays.

There's a pay phone outside on the corner, but the talking part is torn off. There's another one two blocks away, and I'm real happy when I see it, but then I can't reach. It's too high.

The grown-ups don't notice us on Saturdays and Sundays. I'm disappeared, and I can't make anybody find me. There's so many people everywhere, and none of them see me. I keep looking around for Mrs. Harper or Browning, and even Clark Poignant in case he got better enough to be out of his bed, but I don't see them anywhere. What I see are high buildings all right next to each other and lots of cars and stores. There's crowds of people all the time, but no grass. I want to get swung around or chased, but mostly, they can't see me. Only sometimes when they yell for me to get away from there or they laugh without saying why. I don't mind the yelling or laughing because at least somebody's finding you.

• • •

Lyle's allowed to go out on all the days as long as he goes somewhere called the Wheets. That's where he and Kyle used to live and where they don't mind if he's not doing school and if he pretends Kyle is alive. When he comes home at night from their house, he bangs on the door and says, "Let us in, you chuckleheads." We know it's him, and dead Kyle, so we let them in.

• • •

Brooklyn makes us take a bath because Brooklyn says you have to. Lyle smells worse than me because he's eight and bigger than Brooklyn and can get Brooklyn on the floor most of the time when Brooklyn tells him to take a bath. A bath here is

35

different from a bath at Mrs. Harper's. There's only one towel. Brooklyn colored it green, so sometimes, even though we get clean from dirt, we get green on us after we dry off. Lyle and Brooklyn say if I scrub hard enough, I'll uncover the black, but it never happens.

"You white," Lyle says.

"No, I'm not," I say.

"He white," Lyle says to Brooklyn.

"He not black," Brooklyn says.

"I'm not white," I say.

"He mixed," Brooklyn says.

"He not our brother," Lyle says.

"I like his eyes," Brooklyn says, and then he knocks me on the floor.

• • •

Sometimes the lights and the TV don't work. Brooklyn and Lyle get nicer in the dark. We all three get on Brooklyn's bed when the lights and TV don't work, and nobody knocks anybody.

• • •

I write down my numbers on the floor in the corner with a black Magic Marker, but Lyle scribbles over them. I say the numbers over and over in my head, so I won't forget.

"I would like to make a collect call," I say whenever I remember to practice. "I need to make a collect call, please."

• • •

Mrs. Harper said if you need help, you can go to a policeman. Every time Brooklyn sees policemen, he hides real quick. Brooklyn says they'll beat you worse than anyone. He says they'll kill you. When I see policemen, I go the other way.

— ● ● ●

I'm hungry. My stomach is gurgling. Plus also, I want to get caught being bad so I'll get sent back to Mrs. Harper. I take chips and Ding Dongs and run. After a minute, a hand grabs the back of my neck.

"Hold on," a man says, but he's not talking to me yet. He's talking into a cell phone. The cell phone is small and black. It has round white buttons. It has a little black antenna. I want to eat it. I want to wet my pants.

"I need to make a collect call," I tell the man with his hand on my neck.

"Shorty here wants to make a collect call," he shouts into the cell phone. He laughs for a long time. He has gold in his mouth. He takes the Ding Dongs from me.

"I stole them," I say. Maybe he'll send me home.

But instead he tucks his cell phone between his ear and shoulder and rips open my Ding Dongs. He pops one into his mouth and walks away.

— ● ● ●

I like it when Brooklyn has bad dreams, because then I get to share his bed.

"If you tell the dream, you'll never have it again," I tell him. It's one of Mrs. Harper's tricks, and it works real good.

"So?" Brooklyn says. He's warm and smells like cigarettes. His bed is small, so we have to squeeze, but it feels good to get mushed up against another person. A little bit like climbing on Clark Poignant or Browning or getting dried off after a bath by Mrs. Harper.

I'm about to fall asleep when Brooklyn goes, "Dream there a monster."

"What kind of monster?"

"Kind that wearing a mask and chase you to rips out your guts."

"Did it get you?" I ask.

"Almost," Brooklyn says. "But then God kill it."

◆ ◆ ◆

I try real hard to remember my mother. I try to remember her face or her voice. There was a lady Brooklyn and Lyle would call white with toenails painted brown. She rode the bus with me from Mrs. Harper's and then took me in a taxi to an office. Then there was another lady who was my mother. A train underground and Browning's Tootsie Rolls weighing down my back pocket. A street and a door and an elevator going up with a smell a lot like Browning's gin root beer and bad breath. Then there was this apartment and my mother yelling bad words into her cell phone and smacking Lyle on the top of his head. Jamming the cell phone into her pocket and telling me and Lyle and Brooklyn she had to go on an errand and don't open the door for nobody. Leaving and gone.

◆ ◆ ◆

They fight at both next doors. I never see them, but they're grown, and they use a lot of bad words that make me real sure I'll never be able to catch up, be caught, and get sent home. I try, anyway. I start using bad words at Lyle and Brooklyn. When Brooklyn goes to knock me, I grab the ravioli pot and bash him on the head. He falls right on his knees and goes all blank, looking just like one of Mrs. Harper's angels. Then he falls flat on his face, and Lyle crosses his arms.

"You beat him down," Lyle says. I'm still holding the ravioli pot. I put it back on the stove. My hand has some red sauce on it. It matches all the splatters everywhere.

"Hey, Kyle," Lyle says to the empty couch. "America beat down Brooklyn."

"You okay, Brooklyn?" I ask. I touch his butt with my toe. He groans a little bit. I want to smush up against him and tell him *sorry*, but I can't.

He and Lyle get a lot nicer after that.

◆ ◆ ◆

Browning said when you're bad, they send you away. That's why Mrs. Harper sent me away. Because I'm bad. Somebody here would send me away, too, right back to Mrs. Harper, if they saw me being bad, only now I almost forget that's a reason for being bad. I just like it. Plus, Lyle and Brooklyn like it. The more bad I am, the more I don't have to sleep on the gray and black squares.

I pee out the window, but not the air shaft one. The street one. Lyle and Brooklyn like that. I push Lyle out of his bed and give him a fat eye keeping him out. Brooklyn likes that. I tell the store people four blocks over to eat shit so while they're mad at me, Brooklyn can steal bologna and purple bubble gum. I steal a knife and try to make cuts in car tires along the streets. I'm not strong enough, so I steal people's doormats and rip them up instead. I find a brick and smash windows. It's real hard because the windows are higher than me and solid, and the brick is heavy, but I break some, anyway. Brooklyn teaches me how to smoke, only I don't like it, even after I don't cough anymore from it. What I like is lighting the match. I like the blue of the fire at the bottom part of the flame. I like to look at that and then at the yellowy orange above it, and think about when Mrs. Harper would paint the wings or the hair that color.

— — —

"I'll steal a car," Lyle says.

"You don't know how," Brooklyn says. "Plus, you too small."

"I'm bigger than you," Lyle says.

"You a bigger pussy," Brooklyn says. I laugh.

"What is you laughing at?" Brooklyn says. "I'll beat you down."

"No, you won't," I say. "I'm almost as big as you, and I'm not a pussy."

"You used to be," Brooklyn says.

"Used to ain't any use to you," Lyle singsongs.

"Shut up," Brooklyn says, and then he starts giggling.

"Make us some ravioli," I tell Brooklyn. He does.

I steal Magic Markers. I use all the colors. I write my numbers on the walls and the floors. This time, I tell Lyle I'll beat him down if he scribbles it over. I tell him I'll beat down Kyle, too, just in case. When I run out of room, I write my numbers on the stove, the two chair seats, the TV sides and screen, and the outside of the bathtub. Then I write on the sofa bed. The sink. Our clothes.

I have different tricks. Sometimes I write one whole number all in one color. Sometimes I use a different color for each number. Sometimes I do all the sevens one color, and all the threes one color. Brooklyn steals me glitter glue in squeeze tubes, and I make some numbers glitter. When I run out of room in our apartment I start in the hallways. I write my numbers on the floor and the walls. I write them as big as my whole self and as small as my fingernail. I write them on people's doors and on the Plexiglas in the building entranceway that wouldn't break from my brick. I write my numbers for days and days and days. Brooklyn and Lyle like it some but then get bored. When they try to knock me I knock them back. Lyle cries, and Brooklyn stomps away. I'm badder than both of them now.

I run out of room in the hallway. I start on the first elevator. I press the red button that Brooklyn says stops the elevator, so nobody will bother me. I write my numbers as high as I can reach, then

I make Lyle get on his hands and knees so I can stand on his back and write higher. Brooklyn asks me to use all green for the second elevator, so I use all green. Brooklyn likes it. He has to steal a lot of boxes of markers three times in one day. There's only one green in each box. The greens run out fast.

◆ ◆ ◆

You can be bad by saying bad words and stealing and not going to school and wrecking things and beating on people. Plus also, you can just be bad because that's what you are, anyway.

"He crying," Lyle goes. When you're bad nobody much wants you and they send you away.

"So?" Brooklyn goes.

"So, Chucklehead be crying." Now I'm even badder than I ever was at home.

"You best leave his ass alone, or we both going to beat you down good," Brooklyn goes.

Now I'm so so so bad, Mrs. Harper won't ever want me back.

◆ ◆ ◆

Me and Brooklyn have been having us a good time with my numbers all morning in the third elevator.

"Sshhhh," Brooklyn says, because of footsteps. They're loud. Usually we have to stay quiet while we hear curses or somebody kicking at the door before they bang away. But this time we don't hear that. Instead, there's clicking and rattling, and then there's a sliding sound, and a skinny piece of metal sticks through the elevator doors.

42

"Shit," Brooklyn whispers. We watch the skinny piece of metal move back and forth and back and forth, until the doors slide open. A man in a uniform holds the doors open with that skinny piece of metal. He stares at us, and we stare at him. I think he will kill us.

"Well, goddamn," he says. "Goddamn."

Now

I'm mental, but I'm not that mental. It's Brooklyn in here, serving up their nasty food, for real. He's got an apron and some old-lady hair net, and he's bigger than me. He's a man already, but it's him. I stand in the back of the line, and I watch him.

• • •

"How do you get to serve food?" I ask Dr. B.

"What makes you ask?"

"Can you just answer one stupid question?"

"Food serving here is an earned activity. It's reserved for residents in our drug rehabilitation program."

"No shit?"

"No."

"So what drugs are those server dudes on?"

"Nothing, if they're here."

"You know what I mean, man."

"What do you think they're on?"

"How should I know?"

"All right. Cocaine, crack, heroin, ecstasy, special-K, marijuana, alcohol, and other pill, tab, liquid, and inhalant versions of stimulants, depressants, and hallucinogens."

"Which building are they in? And don't ask me what building I think they're in, or I swear——"

"All right," Dr. B. says. "J building."

J building.

"You want to play War?" I go.

"Aren't you tired of War?" he goes.

Sometimes, he's funny.

—•—•—•—

Brooklyn's serving breakfast, and I keep my head down over my tray. I don't want him to see me yet.

—•—•—•—

"You got a brother?"

"Do you?"

"I asked first."

"Hmm," Dr. B. says. He looks like he's thinking. "What would you guess?"

"If I knew, I wouldn't be asking," I tell him.

"I didn't ask if you knew," he goes. "I asked what you'd guess."

"Yeah," I tell him. "You got a brother."

"You think?"

"You and him talk on the phone, right?" Dr. B. stays still. "You talk on the phone and drink beers and all that on the weekends."

"You think we spend time together and get along well."

"Yeah, but when you were small, I bet he beat the shit out of you."

"Really?" Dr. B. goes.

"Yup," I tell him.

• • •

He's serving dinner. He's got some kind of mark, some scar near his mouth. I hold my head up and look at him straight on, but he's staring at the damn creamed corn, and he doesn't see me. That's my brother.

• • •

I skip group and watch Ping-Pong, and I get in my bed, and I get back out and sit in front of the TV, the real one, and then I walk circles around the rec room and squash a Ping-Pong ball that gets in the way of my foot and ignore those guys yelling at me, and I walk up and down the main hall with the yellow and red trees out the windows, and I remember about it.

Those gray and black squares and that air shaft and I Declare War. The smell of regular cigarettes and the way I got badder and badder and badder and that time he had his nightmare.

• • •

"Aren't you going to say something?" I go.

"I was waiting for you to begin."

"You always wait for me. Why don't you start, for a change?"

"Well, what would you like me to say?" Dr. B. asks.

"You know what?" I tell him.

"What?"

"You are some big mystery."

He smiles. "And so are you."

I don't remember his ass smiling before. I was feeling all right, but I don't like smiling. I don't want him smiling.

—•—•—•—

Brooklyn never looks up. He just wears that old-lady hair net, and that white apron, and those stupid plastic gloves, and he never looks up.

—•—•—•—

"I asked you to stop staring at me."

"What's going on, America?"

"Nothing's going on. What's your problem?"

"I'm not aware of having a problem."

"You've got so many goddamn problems, doc, I wouldn't even know where all to start."

"Is that right?"

"That's right. So get out of my face."

Then

I'm in a room with no windows. A wrinkled lady asks me to write my name. I don't know how.

"Eat shit, bitch."

"Do you know what *eat shit, bitch* means?" she asks. I'm so surprised to hear some wrinkled lady in a room with no windows say bad words that I forget to figure out if I know what they mean. She asks me to draw a picture of my family.

I draw my numbers first. I draw them all over the paper, everywhere. It takes a long time, but the wrinkled lady doesn't tell me to hurry up. When the numbers are done, I draw the picture part over them. A cement rectangle flat to the ground at an open front door, flower-filled clay plots, and shelves lined with angels. I draw Mrs. Harper looking out an upstairs window into the backyard with me and Browning playing ball. I draw butterflies flying around and a footprint in one corner of the cement rectangle.

Then I get confused. "Where do Brooklyn and Lyle go?" I ask.

"They'll go to people who will take care of them," the lady says. "Maybe to the Wheets." I don't get it. I look at my drawing, trying to figure it out. "Tell me about your picture," the lady says.

"Eat shit, bitch," I say.

* * *

I'm in another room. The wrinkled lady walked me here through lots of elevators and hallways and doors and steps. She told me to sit in this chair, and then she left. I swing my legs for a while, then I take a pen off the table next to me. I get out of my chair and lean down over it to write my numbers on the seat. The pen is slippery, harder to hold than a Magic Marker or even a crayon, but the ink is blue and comes out good.

"Jesus," I hear, and there's a man with no hair and a newspaper in his hand. He's looking at me. "You're him." He shakes the paper a little bit, holding it out. It's got a lot of pictures of Brooklyn and Lyle's building. The inside of the apartment, the hallways, the elevators. You can see my numbers everywhere, all over. I did a good job. "Jesus," the man says. He's looking at my numbers on the chair seat. He looks back and forth at me, at my numbers, at the newspaper. A phone rings on a desk. The phone makes me real nervous, but I don't know why. I want it, and I want to get away, too. It rings again, and the man picks it up. A white woman with a girl my size walks in.

"Is that boy Chinese?" the girl says.

I'm in a bed all to myself. A real bed. It smells clean. There's three beds lined up next to mine. I'm full with chicken and noodles and Jell-O salad. I'm clean from a shower and a fresh towel that I didn't have to share.

"She don't get mad if you pee yourself," somebody tells me.

There's a night-light on the floor by the door. I watch my fingers spread apart in front of me. I make them wiggle and bend. I bring both my hands together, like the way you pray. Then I open them again, like a book. I start to draw my numbers in the air, but then I stop.

There's stairs. I'm sitting on the top of one. In the middle. People have to ask me to move so they can get by. They ask polite, not like Brooklyn or Lyle. They don't say, *Get out my way.* They say, *Excuse me, please.*

"You want mine?" a boy says. He's handing me an oatmeal-raisin cookie. "I only eat chocolate chip."

I take his cookie, but I don't eat it. I pick out the raisins and smush them on the top stair.

Mrs. Harper said it about raisins. And chocolate chips and nuts.

Real meaning is in the smaller things, she'd say. She said it about the buckle part of her favorite belt. The smell of the air after Browning mowed the lawn. She said it the time the lights went out and the flashlight batteries were dead, and we had to use candles, and the flames were like winking stars all over the house. *Real meaning is in the smaller things,* she would tell me. She said it when Clark Poignant brought little paper-wrapped soaps from the hotel where he'd stayed on a trip; she said it every time she filled up her tulip vases with fresh water.

• • •

There's a playground. The grandmother makes me go on it after too many days on the stairs. I stand there and watch the other kids playing tag. My throat gets a headache. I try to go back inside, but the grandmother won't let me. She makes me stay out.

"Come on, America," someone yells. "Come on."

I stand still, but they chase me, anyway. Someone taps my shoulder and jumps away. His hand is hard and warm on my back. Something swims around in my blood, making it so I can't move.

"Got you! You're it!" he yells. He tags me again. It's not a knock-you-down, beat-you-down hand, but a tag-game hand. A find-you hand. Find. You.

"Got you!"

I scream. My hide-and-seek scream. My tag-and-tickle and you-can't-catch-me scream. I scream and scream and scream.

They try to make me stop, but I can't. They get the grandmother, and she tries to make me stop, but I can't.

I can't stop screaming.

I try to wake up. But the covers are too heavy, and when I'm in a chair or walking somewhere, the air is too heavy. Sometimes I want to write my numbers, and sometimes I want to change the channel on the TV, but it's all too heavy. I want to remember something, but it's too far away. Everything tastes like ravioli.

I'm in a room with Mike. He's a man, but he sits on the floor and has a lot of toys. Toys good for seven-year-olds like me. A garage with trucks. Play-Doh. Puppets. A mushy ball you can squeeze or throw through its own hoop. Crayons and Magic Markers and paper. I've been here with him before. Maybe a lot of times. I know the dump truck and table and the ripped part on the chair and Mike. I know his front tooth that sticks out over the one next to it. I don't feel so tired anymore. The air isn't so heavy. I remember how I'm bad. There's a reason it is good to be bad. I'll throw the toys, or break them, or write my numbers on the walls, but I'm too tired.

"What would you like to do?" Mike asks me. I'm too tired. I want to tell him, *eat shit,* but I'm too tired. "Maybe the next time we meet, you'll feel like playing something," Mike says. "You won't be taking any medicine anymore, and the medicine makes you feel sort of slow. So the next time, maybe you won't feel so slow." Next time.

It's not so heavy anymore, and I remember leaving places and going places and getting places. There was the bus from Mrs. Harper's with the lady and then a taxi with the lady to an office. There was my mother and me on a train underground and then walking to a building with an elevator that took us high to Brooklyn's apartment. There was the sofa bed and the green towel and War and dead Kyle. There was me and Brooklyn and Lyle in an ambulance to a hospital and a wheelchair in a hospital with a nurse wheeling me away from Brooklyn and Lyle to a place where she gave me a shower to another place where they poked me and stuck needles in me and another wheelchair to a place where they put me in a bed and gave me soup. Then there was leaving the hospital with a whole different lady in a car to a building and a different, different lady in the building walking me through halls and steps and doors and then another car with a man to the place where the grandmother didn't get mad if you peed your bed, and then my bed here and my own feet walking me to Mike's room.

"Is this a hospital?" I ask Mike.

"I see you're feeling better," he says.

"Do I live here now?"

"This is one kind of hospital," Mike says. "And you'll stay here for a while longer, probably. Do you remember me telling you what happened?"

"No."

"What happened was, you got out of control a few days after you arrived at a foster home. You got so out of control that it was like you got very sick, and we're helping you get better, and you've been here for a lot of weeks."

There's a phone on the floor. But it's plastic and not attached to anything. Also, it's pink, which is pussy. Mike hands me a piece of paper and a can full of crayons and Magic Markers.

"You want to draw?" he says. I'm not tired anymore. I rip up the paper and throw the can and the crayons and the markers across the room. It's good to be bad. Mike stays quiet and doesn't hit me or send me away.

We sit for a long time, and I want to write my numbers. There's a pencil on the table. I pick it up and start writing. I write straight on the table. You're not supposed to write on tables, but Mike doesn't care. It's hard to get the pencil to show, but I do a lot of layers and make it show, anyway. I write my numbers. I write and write and write. I'm covering the table.

"That's a lot of numbers," Mike says. "A whole lot of numbers." I keep writing. "What do they mean?" Mike says after a while. I keep writing. "Who taught you those numbers?" Mike says. *Who taught you those numbers?* I stop writing. I look at the pink phone. Mike sees me looking. "Would you like to make a call?"

"I need to make a collect call," I tell him.

"A collect call?" he says. I nod.

"Okay." He points to the phone.

"It's not real," I tell him.

"That's right," he says.

"I need to make a real collect call." Mike looks at me for a long time. Maybe he has a phone. Maybe he has a phone somewhere else. I'm thinking there are phones in hospitals. Maybe I've even seen one, but everything was too heavy. "I need to make a collect call," I say. "Please."

Mike is still looking at me. He looks for a long time again. Then he looks at the phone. Then he looks at my numbers. He looks hard at the numbers. He looks hard at me. "Is there someone at the other end of the numbers?" he finally asks, quiet.

Mrs. Harper and Clark Poignant and Browning. Mrs. Harper and Clark Poignant and Browning. Mrs. Harper.

Mrs. Harper. Mrs.HarperMrsHarperMrsHarper. *I see you!*

"Mrs. Harper," I say. Mike clears his throat. He clears it again.

"Mrs. Harper," Mike says.

"Please," I say. "Please."

Now

You sit in here long enough and you get to floating. You throw down your cards and scoop them up, and you do the chant when you get War, and you float. Dr. B. talks some and stays quiet some, and you hear him some, but then you don't, and flashes squeeze through, and you get sick of trying to make them stop. You just give up after a while, and let them come.

● ● ●

"Don't do that," I go. "Game's not over."

"Our time is up for today," Dr. B. goes.

"I know what time we're done here, doc," I go. "I'm just saying, keep our piles straight, and put them somewhere safe so we can finish the game right next session."

"Where would be safe?"

"Put my pile in that top drawer and your pile in the bottom one."

"All right."

"No messing with them when I'm not here, man."

"You don't want me to cheat."

"You better not."

"I won't."

"And if any of your other chuckleheads need to play Go Fish or some shit, you just buy some other deck."

"I won't let anyone else interfere with our game."

"That's what I'm saying."

"Okay."

They change the group room, so I can't watch the TV in the wall. I don't care because now I'm listening. They don't know I'm listening, but I am. It's the only way to know what all is going on.

"He earned, like, a ton of privileges," this red-haired kid is telling everybody. He's got some cousin over there in J building he's all worked up about. "And he got a visit, and then his urine tested dirty, so then he had to detox all over again."

"Thirty days?" somebody asks.

"Twenty-eight," red hair goes. "When he's done, he's got to start all over again over there."

"Damn," some other dude says.

Maybe that's why I haven't seen Brooklyn for a while. Maybe he lost all his privileges from a dirty urine he got somehow, and now he's in that isolation over in detox, out there in J building.

I wake up, and my shoulder hurts real bad. I fix myself straight flat out, but I can't sleep. My shoulder's too goddamn sore. I throw my arm down there over the side of my bed and feel around until I find my stupid pillow. I put it up under my head and roll over on my front and put the pillow down under my neck some, and the next thing I know, it's morning already.

－•－•－•

"You always have the same questions, man. What's it like this, what's it like that, what's it like the other thing."

"Hmm."

"You should let me ask a question once in a while."

"I should?"

"Yeah. You live in a big house?"

"What's big?"

"You're shitting me, right?"

"Well, no. Big can mean different things to different people. I need to know what big is, in your mind. And also, I'm wondering how you imagine my house to be."

"You've got a problem, man," I go. "You've got an asking questions problem."

We stay quiet a minute. Then he goes, "You know how we've talked about how it's difficult for you to begin?"

"Yup."

"I guess what's difficult for me is not to ask questions."

"Well, all right. Let's talk about that."

"What interests you about that?"

"Damn, doc. You just can't help yourself, can you?"

⋅ ✷ ✷ ✷ ⋅

I count. It's not any twenty-eight days. It's not even thirty. It's thirty-eight fucking days, and he's still gone. No stupid gloves. No apron. No old-lady hair net. No Brooklyn. No goddamn nothing.

⋅ ✷ ✷ ✷ ⋅

They come and go while we play War. They sign their stupid contracts, and they take their stupid meds, and they show up to their stupid sessions, and they talk their butts off in group, and then they get visitors, and then they go. Nobody stays here except me. Everybody else has a place. They have a mother or a grandfather or a foster family or long-term residential or some group home somewhere. There's always somebody to take them, but not me. I'm here the longest because everywhere else is booked full like some kind of Hilton hotel, or I'm the wrong age or in the wrong district, and I don't have any people. Mrs. Harper's in some nursing home somewhere, if she hasn't croaked, but they don't take fifteen-year-old boys in nursing homes, and who says she'd want me, anyway? Old ladies have no use for boys. That's what Browning always said. Boys just aggravate old ladies and tire them out. Especially me, because everybody knows I'm bad.

She never should have taken my ass back.

⋅ ✷ ✷ ✷ ⋅

I don't ask him again, but I float during War, and this is how I see it. When Dr. B. goes home, sometimes his brother is there, just visiting, sitting on this big front porch, drinking beers. B. lives with his mom, and she's got dinner all waiting on the table already. She watches from the window and then opens the front door and walks out quick to the front porch to wait with his brother, right when B.'s pulling up in his Jeep out there in the driveway. It takes him a real long time to get over to them on that porch, because he's got a house so damn big, it's five whole minutes just to cross the yard.

Then

There's streamers on the front door. There's a ribbon sign with words I can't read. There's balloons. The lady who drove me all the way here tells me I can get out of the car now. I walk up to the cement-slab rectangle and set my high-top flat over that corner footprint, and Mrs. Harper's door opens. Browning is there, holding Mrs. Harper's arm. Browning's bigger than he was two years ago, and Mrs. Harper is skinnier. Her neck is bent forward, and her face is still.

"America," Mrs. Harper says.

"Careful," Browning tells her. She leans down and pulls me in for a squeeze. Her bones feel little. I want her to get me tighter and tighter and tighter, and she does, but I'm real scared she'll turn her back when she lets go because I'm bad.

"I'm sorry," I tell her.

"America," she says.

Browning moved in right after I got sent away. His room is the room that used to be mine. Now it's ours. It smells sweet from the brown cigarettes he still smokes. He's not allowed to light them anywhere in the house except our room because the smoke gets on Mrs. Harper's nerves. He takes care of her because she got old when I was gone, and she's sick a lot. Browning is fat, and he switched his drink from gin in root beer to regular beer and Jim Beam. His breath stinks all the time, and when we play Wiffle ball, he doesn't pitch as good as he used to. But he talks to me a lot. He's still the one who tells me everything. He tells me Mrs. Harper missed me more than anything, and so did he. He tells me Clark Poignant died a month after I left, and between losing me and him, Mrs. Harper got real ill and got better but was never the same. He explains it took too long for them to find me after I never came home that Saturday. I got lost in the system. My case manager got fired and her boss had to go to court, but I was still lost. A long time later, Mrs. Harper saw the story about the boy with the numbers in the paper, but she didn't look close enough at the picture to see the numbers were her own. Browning tells me that when she got the call from Mike, she cried and cried and cried and cried. Browning says we'll be a team now: me and him, taking care of Mrs. Harper.

He tells me he's glad I'm back, because he's been real lonely.

Mrs. Harper says I've learned a lot of vocabulary and a lot of it is bad, extra especially for a person just barely eight years old. She washes my mouth out with soap.

"Get off!" I yell, and Browning pokes his head into the bathroom to smack the side of my head. His hand is thick, and it hurts.

"Don't you hit him," Mrs. Harper tells Browning, and then she turns her back on me and walks out of the bathroom. The soap tastes like plastic-flavored throw up, and my ear burns.

• • •

"What does this say?" Mrs. Harper asks. She's pointing to the new cardboard box full of angels waiting on the cement rectangle. She only gets one box a month these days because her arthritis doesn't let her paint too much anymore.

"This end up," I say, lifting the box for her. But I didn't read it, I just knew.

"You're guessing," she says. She and the state decided she's going to teach me to read before I start second grade.

Inside, and I put the box down in her workroom.

She points to a paint bottle. "Don't guess," she says. "Sound it out."

"Indian."

"Indigo." She sighs, like she thinks I'm stupid. I throw Indian on the floor and watch the paint splatter everywhere, like blue blood. "America!" Mrs. Harper scolds.

"What'd he do this time?" Browning calls from somewhere.

"Didn't do shit!" I yell as loud as I know how.

Browning runs in and smacks my head twice, and Mrs. Harper looks at me hard, turns her back, and doesn't speak to me for a whole day. When she needs me to pass the pepper or get washed for bed or to change the channel, she tells Browning to tell me. She makes me invisible even when I'm right in front of her.

I'm bad. I can't help it. It's just what I am. Bad.

◦ ◦ ◦

I'm lying on my stomach in bed. I hear a dragging sound, mixed up with creaking, and when it gets closer, I know it's Mrs. Harper with her walker. It takes her forever to get to the side of my bed, and I stay still, pretending to be asleep. She hasn't touched me since she washed out my mouth, and her little, light hand in the middle of my back is nice. I stay real still as her hand moves up and down. I'm trying to think of what to say, but it's hard. I could say I'm not really asleep, or I could tell her about how Brooklyn never had his nightmare again after I told him her trick, but then maybe she'll stop. I don't want her to stop. I want her to sit here, petting my back all night long. But right as I decide to whisper to her, Browning is at the bedroom door, going, "Come on, now." Her hand stops on my back, but it stays flat, and Browning says, "Let's get you ready for bed."

Her hand pats me, and then it goes away.

Browning finds me out by the chain-link fence.

"Where'd you get that lighter?" he asks. I shrug. "Did you steal it?"

"No," I lie. I stole it right under Mrs. Harper's nose at the 7-Eleven.

"Put it out," he says. I ignore him and watch the flame. Real meaning is in the smaller things.

Browning snatches the lighter from me.

"Give it back," I say.

"I'm going to teach you how to read," he says. He fixes a cigarette between his lips. "After you learn enough to start school, I'll give you back the lighter." I stare mad at him. He pulls a stack of homemade flash cards from his back pocket and huffs his way down to his butt on the grass. He sure did get fat. "Sit down," he tells me.

"I don't have to."

I wait for him to smack me, but he doesn't this time. He flicks my lighter on and touches the flame to his cigarette. He blows the smoke out the side of his mouth, away from my face, but I can still smell the sweetness.

"Listen," Browning says. "Mrs. Harper doesn't know I'm going to teach you. So don't tell her." He waits a second, inhaling, but I won't look at him. "She wouldn't like the way I'm going to teach you, so you and me are going to keep it to our own two selves. Just our secret. Okay?" When I don't answer, he holds up the first card.

"That's the same way Mrs. Harper does it," I tell him.

"Nope," Browning says. "You'll see. Try it."

"Ssss," I go. "Sss huh."

"Remember what sound *s* and *h* make," he says. He licks his lips and taps out some ash while I think hard.

"Shh," I say.

He nods.

"Sshhiiii."

He nods again.

"Shit," I go.

"That's what I'm trying to say."

"You can't write that on a card!" I go.

"I can do whatever I want," he says. He holds up another one.

"Fff," I start. Then I stop.

"Keep going," Browning says.

"I can't," I tell him. "That's going to be the f-word."

"What, all of a sudden you're afraid to say the f-word?" he asks me.

"Are all the cards bad words?" I whisper.

Browning raises his eyebrows and nods toward the house. "Ssshhh," he says.

He uses other words, too, mixed in with the bad ones. Like our names, and the different names of his drinks. Malt, vodka, gin, beer, wine. He uses the way we all talk. Don't raise your voice. Clean it up. Don't you dare. Can somebody get the phone?

Mrs. Harper doesn't know what we're up to, but she likes that I'm doing better with her own flash

cards and with the *TV Guide*. I can read a few sen-
tences from it now, and plus, I can read some of her
mail.

"'Dear Sylvia,'" I read. "Who's that?"

"Who's what?" Mrs. Harper says.

"Who's Sylvia?" She starts to laugh.

"What?" I say.

"Who's Sylvia!" she hoots.

"What?" I say. She's laughing at me. She hates
me and thinks I'm stupid.

"I'm Sylvia." She's got tears coming out the
corners of her eyes. She wipes at them with the tail of
the scarf she's started wearing over her hair. I never
thought of her as anything but Mrs. Harper. That's
all anybody ever calls her. I'm trying to stay mad, but
it's hard with her laughing like that, it's hard with
her suddenly being Sylvia. It's making me want to
laugh, too. "You always had such a nice smile," Mrs.
Harper tells me, and she pats at her cheeks and her
neck with her scarf tails. "Real nice." Then she starts
laughing all over again, and I don't mind so much
anymore.

■ ■ ●

Mostly, Browning teaches me by the chain-link
fence where Mrs. Harper thinks we're just hanging
out, or in our room after she's asleep. Browning
squeezes in next to me in my bed and dangles his
arm around my shoulders while we practice, and
sometimes that makes me forget feeling so bad and
mean. Browning says not to care what everybody
else thinks because the truth is, I'm plenty smart,

and I'm a good listener, too. He says thank God I came home because he sure did need some fresh company.

When I tell him I think Mrs. Harper liked me better before I left, he doesn't argue but just stays quiet and blows smoke rings, so then I know it must be true that she doesn't love me anymore. I don't let Browning hear me cry about it because only pussies cry, and besides, she's old and I don't care all that much, anyway. I have Browning, and he's all I need.

— ● ● ●

They put me in special ed. There's only seven other kids in my class, and all the other classes are a lot bigger and have regular people who aren't supposed to be dumb and bad. There's a girl who sits next to me who reminds me of Brooklyn, even though she's a girl. Her name is Liza. When I tell her to eat shit, she goes, "Anyplace, anytime."

They all read better than me, and this one kid, Billy, says he'll help me, and when I tell him what he can do with his stupid help, he starts screaming, "I *hate* you! I *hate* you!" and the teacher puts me in a time-out. She's always pushing her glasses back up her nose, and she doesn't yell, but she talks soft, like she's far away inside of herself.

"What an unusual name," she tells me. I pretend not to hear her.

Liza says, "He looks like a America."

Everyone laughs, and I try to hit her, but she dodges. She's fast. "It's good, dummy," Liza says.

"America's supposed to be for everybody, and you look like everybody."

"He's not black," some other kid says.

"Shut up," I tell him.

Liza rolls her eyes. "It's *good*," she says. "You want to get married?"

- ● ● ●

Mrs. Harper goes to bed way early now, and I sit on a stool near to her feet and read. The teacher gave me some books, but Mrs. Harper likes magazines better. I always want to say *d* instead of divorce and *s* instead of sensational and *c* instead of celebrity because it takes so long to sound them out, but Mrs. Harper won't let me. She makes me work out the whole word every time, and then finally, after a lot of magazines and a lot of days, I know what *divorce* and *sensational* and *celebrity* look like as soon as I see them. I know she's real happy about that because she lets her teeth show a little, and she says, *That's right, America. Uh-huh. That's just right.* It's real nice.

Browning doesn't give me back the lighter I stole, because he lost it. He gives me another lighter instead that has a naked lady on it.

"Don't tell Mrs. Harper," he says, and then he winks.

Now

I get seconds just to see if maybe he's back there behind those swinging doors. He's not, though. Some other dudes are serving. Brooklyn's ass is good and gone.

• • •

Dr. B. tells me it's probably real hard for me to trust anyone, especially maybe him for some reason, only he's not sure, and do I think that might be true.

I'm way up high.

"America," Dr. B. is going. "America."

Way up high.

"America!"

"What?" I go, falling back down right into my chair.

"What just happened there?"

"Nothing," I tell him.

"You looked like you went away somewhere."

"Nah," I tell him. "You're looking at me, aren't you? I'm right here."

"No," Dr. B. goes. "You went away." I try to get back up there, but I can't. He's looking at me, he's seeing me, and I can't go. "America," Dr. B. says. "What's going on?"

"Nothing," I say. "Step off."

It was cool and clean and icy and snow everywhere. It was way up high and real nice.

"I think we were getting to something important, and then you went somewhere."

"Would you shut up with that?" I go. "I'm right here!"

"Not a minute ago," he tells me. "You were somewhere else."

"Don't know what the hell you're talking about, man."

"I think you know."

"You're out of your tree, doc. I swear."

"I think you're afraid you're out of your tree."

"Is our time up yet? This is boring."

"You know exactly when our time is up, America."

"Ah, shit."

"It's called dissociation." He's getting on my nerves, bad. "A lot of people do it when something's happening in the here and now that's upsetting to them. A lot of people find a way to go outside of themselves. They use their minds to take themselves away because it feels safer that way."

"Step off, man."

"It doesn't make anybody crazy, America."

"Didn't you hear me? I said, step off!"

"I heard you."

"So shut up, then."

— • • —

Either way, you lose. You play War, and you get that floating and those flashes. You don't play War, and you get to talking and then you shoot up high. I hate these damn sessions. I hate Dr. B.

— • • —

"Who messed with our game?"

"I must have done it when I was looking for something in my drawers."

"You messed it all up."

"I'm sorry, America."

"Why weren't you more careful, man?"

"I don't know. It was an accident."

"If you don't want to play, why don't you just say so?"

"Hmm."

"You suck."

"You're really mad at me."

"You fucking suck, man."

— • • —

They get on me in group.

"How long has he been here, anyway?" some kid goes.

"America, do you want to answer that?" the group lady goes.

"Do you want to eat shit?" I go.

"That just cost you rec room tonight," she goes.

Who needs to watch Ping-Pong, anyway? I go to

72

the main hall instead. I walk up and down, looking out the windows, watching the last of those damn leaves dripping off those trees.

• • •

I'm leaning my head way over the back of the chair. "Whatever."

"You seemed pretty invested in finishing this game last week."

"I said, 'whatever,' doc." Those little gray soldiers are aiming straight for my upside-down face. Every last one of them.

"You were so angry when you saw I'd gotten our piles mixed up."

"So?" They look like they're getting ready to shoot my eyes out.

"So you've changed your mind."

"Yup."

"You don't care about the game anymore."

I sit up. "Nope."

"I guess this means we're not playing today, then."

"Well, congratulations, genius. You guessed right."

Then

She can't cook anymore, but Browning says no problem because nine is plenty old enough to learn how to fix a good meal. So I read out the recipes, and Browning and me follow the directions, and Mrs. Harper lies on the living room couch and calls out the parts they don't write down anywhere.

"Squeeze out the vegetables after you shred them. They go watery, otherwise!" she'll yell. Or she'll go, "The back left burner smokes up some! Be careful it doesn't set off the fire alarm!"

"The best chefs are men," Browning likes to say.

At school, Liza says that's true. "Make me some cookies," she says. "M&M chip."

"Maybe," I tell her.

"Just the green ones. The green ones make you horny."

She still reminds me all the time of Brooklyn. Sometimes I wonder about him and Lyle. I wonder what they would think of my naked lady lighter and Liza. She could beat down Lyle, I think, but maybe not Brooklyn. Me and her get into a fight when I start to catch up to her at reading, and she pins me down, but instead of smashing my nose, she kisses my mouth.

● ● ●

I like the way Browning takes care of things. I like the stuff he tells me, too. He talks to me like I'm grown, and everything.

"Mrs. Harper tells me I need a job," Browning says sometimes, after we're done reading, and we're just hanging out, squished together in my bed. "She doesn't know taking care of her is a full-time job, you know?"

"Yeah," I say. He turns his head sideways so I can start up his cigarette with my naked lady lighter. I've lost count of how many I've had, but between him smoking and me watching the flame, we use up lighters pretty fast.

"She doesn't know how hard it is looking after an old lady."

"Yeah," I say. "There's lots of stuff to do."

"My point exactly," Browning says, inhaling. "Like shopping and cooking and taking her to doctor's appointments and keeping her clean and whatnot."

"Yeah," I say, feeling sorry for him.

"It's not like I have a personal life anymore, either," Browning says. "I haven't had me any in forever." He sighs a stream of smoke toward the foot of the bed.

"Yeah," I say.

He laughs. "You don't even know what I'm talking about," he says.

"Yes, I do," I tell him. "You're talking about sex."

"What do you know about sex?" he tells me.

"I've got a girlfriend," I tell him, thinking about Liza.

"Oh, yeah?" he says. "You two getting it on already?" I shrug. I think about her lips on my lips. "I got a sore muscle," Browning says. He rolls onto his stomach. "Give me a rub, man." I sit on his butt and rub the back of his neck. "A little to the left." He taps his ash into an empty beer can on the floor. "Yeah. Right there."

◦ ◦ ◦

Liza and me cut school and go to the 7-Eleven. Liza steals gum, and then we stand by the Dumpster outside. Liza chews her gum for two seconds and then takes it out of her mouth. "You want some?" she asks, holding it up.

"Give me a new piece," I tell her.

"Take this one."

"It's nasty," I tell her. "Give me a fresh one."

"Don't be a baby," she says. I take it from her and pop it in my mouth. "Kiss me," she says, and she puts her mouth on mine. The next thing I know, she's got the piece of gum back. She blows a bubble with it. "Can you blow a bubble inside a bubble?" she asks.

"Can you?" I go.

"We know I can. Can you?"

"We know I can. Can you?"

"Stop it, America."

"Stop it, America."

"Shut up!" she yells. She hits me in the chest. I try to hit her back, but she punches me, and I run. She chases me.

"Get off!" I'm yelling.

"Don't run away!" she shouts, but I keep going, and when I turn around to see if it's safe, she's on her knees in the 7-Eleven parking lot, crying.

"What's the matter?" I call. She keeps crying, and I want her to stop, so I get next to her and try patting her head, and then I end up hugging her, and she hugs me back. She smells like dishwash soap.

● ● ●

When I get home, Mrs. Harper's on the couch downstairs with the TV off.

"You're in trouble," Browning tells me from the kitchen.

"You left out of school today," Mrs. Harper announces.

"No, I didn't," I say.

"Don't you lie to me," Mrs. Harper says.

"I thought we had a half day," I tell her.

"Your lip is bleeding," Mrs. Harper says.

"No, it's not," I say.

"America," Mrs. Harper says. I catch sight of the workroom behind her. There's only a couple of angels on the shelves, and the paint lids have crusty rings all around their edges. "Do you realize that you are in trouble?" she asks me. Then she closes her eyes. "Browning," she says. "Take care of it, please."

I help him chop vegetables to go with the roasted chicken.

"I don't care if you cut school," he says. "But Mrs. Harper does. If you piss her off too much, she's going to get sicker. Do you want to make her sicker?"

"I don't care," I lie.

Browning sighs. "School will be better when you catch up all the way." The rice starts to boil over, and he lowers the heat on the burner and takes the top off the saucepan. "We've got to get your reading on a higher level. More on a man level than a boy level. You're still reading kiddie stuff."

I scrape a fork down the sides of a zucchini the way Browning showed me, to make fancy ridges in the slices. "Mrs. Harper's magazines aren't kiddie," I say. "And I read chapter books in school."

"Yeah, well, our flash cards are kiddie, and so is that chapter garbage your teacher has you reading."

"Nuh-uh," I say, even though it's true.

"And you've got to relax a little," Browning tells me. "You're too tense, man. It's hard to learn when you're tense."

"How am I going to relax?"

Browning smiles. "It'll be another secret," he tells me. "Because Mrs. Harper wouldn't like it."

"Like what?" I say.

He hands me a beer. "Try it," he says.

It tastes like the smell of his bad breath. I spit it right into the sink. Browning sighs. He pulls out his vodka from his special shelf, unscrews the cap, and hands the bottle to me. The little swallow I take burns my throat. I cough. Browning takes a bottle of Coke out of the refrigerator and mixes some of that in a glass with some vodka. "Try that."

It mostly tastes like Coke. "That's okay," I say.

"Okay," Browning says.

⚬ ⚬ ⚬

He gives me a vodka and Coke every night. After dinner I feel warm and lazy. It's nice. It's relaxing.

"He needs milk," Mrs. Harper says when she sees the Coke at dinnertime.

"He drinks milk every day at school for lunch," Browning goes, winking at me.

Liza is jealous. "Bring me some," she says. "Bring a bottle in your knapsack and then keep it in your locker."

I ask Browning, but he says no. He says if I get caught, it'll make Mrs. Harper sicker.

"Sorry," I tell Liza.

"Can you steal it from him?" Liza asks.

"No," I say.

"Chicken," Liza snorts.

"Shut up."

"Lucky," Liza says. "You're so lucky."

⚬ ⚬ ⚬

I'm in the middle of reading about an actor who's divorcing from a lady who used to be the wife of a governor when Mrs. Harper tells me to stop. So I stop.

"America," she says.

"Yeah?"

"Do you remember Clark Poignant?"

"Yeah," I say.

"What do you remember about him?"

"He liked to mow his lawn in circles instead of rows," I tell her.

She smiles. "Yes, he did."

"Once I was supposed to be sleeping but I came downstairs, and he was watching our TV," I tell her. Then I wait for her to be mad, but she keeps smiling.

"The Home Shopping Network," she says.

"He liked those little cups. Those silver-colored ones."

"Pewter," Mrs. Harper says. "They were pewter cups, and he always wanted to buy them."

"Yeah," I say.

"Real meaning is in the smaller things," Mrs. Harper says, real soft.

I try to think of the very smallest thing. "He liked that tie clip they had, too," I tell her. "The red, white, and blue flag one."

"Let's watch," Mrs. Harper says. She likes me again. I know it. I go to turn on the TV, but Browning comes in and reminds me I've got to wash dishes and take out the garbage.

"If you bother her too much," Browning whispers to me over the trash bag, "you're going to tire her all out."

I can hear the Home Shopping Network from the other room.

"Maybe she's lonely," I tell Browning. I want to say, *I think she misses me a little.*

"Nah," he says. "I doubt it."

Summer school is the same as regular school, only it's half a day, and we take field trips once a week. Billy's mother is the parent chaperone for the Mount Everest IMAX movie.

"You know," Liza tells Billy while we're waiting in line for tickets, "you're a lot calmer when your mom's around."

Billy smiles, and we let him sit next to us. We pick the highest row, and it's a long, deep way to the bottom of the movie theater, with all these curving lines of red seats and dark seat backs and bobbing helmet-goggled heads. Once the movie starts, you feel real small and low to the ground one second, and then real huge and high in the air the next. This avalanche falls right on top of you, and as soon as you duck, you're right back in your seat, and then you're looking out across the whole world with snow all around and under you, and you almost feel cold, and you almost want to jump because it sort of seems like you could fly.

"A bunch of people died up there all at once during this storm," Liza whispers. "The air gets so thin, it makes your brain get dumb, and you can't think right, and you walk right over the edge of those snow cliffs."

"Nuh-uh," Billy says.

"Yuh-huh," Liza says. "And even if you live through it, the frostbite turns your skin black until it falls off. Whole arms and legs fall off. Bang. Just like that."

"Shut up," I tell them, because I like being small and big and close and far all at the same time. I like the way the movie makes you feel like a little bug one minute, and like God the next. I like the way the clouds and the snow look the same, the way the spikes in the climbers' boots and the red of their coats are as sharp as the glare of the sun on the ice. I like the way it makes me feel dizzy and safe, both at the same time, when they show us what that mountain looks like under our own feet and over our heads. I like it better than just about anything, and I want to watch it in peace.

● ● ●

"America says you stopped painting angels because you're too tired," Liza says.

"Is that right?" Mrs. Harper goes. She's all propped up on her pillows.

"Yep," Liza says. "That's too bad, because me and America think you paint them really beautiful."

"Is that what you think, America?" Mrs. Harper asks. I shrug. I'm afraid Liza being over will wear Mrs. Harper right out and make her sicker, just like Browning's always warning me. But Liza says old people need company sometimes, and then she just showed up on our cement rectangle and rang and rang our bell, even after I told her not to.

"How come nobody calls you anything but Mrs. Harper, anyway?" Liza asks.

"I happen to have a friend who calls me Sylvia," Mrs. Harper says.

"Only in letters," I go.

"Everybody calls you Mrs. Harper," Liza goes. "Even Browning."

"I guess that's true," Mrs. Harper says, but then she doesn't say why.

"America says you don't like him so much anymore because he's dumb and bad."

"Liza!" I go. She's not supposed to say that.

"America is not dumb or bad, either one," Mrs. Harper says.

"Duh," Liza says.

"I never said that," I lie.

"It's not true," Mrs. Harper says. Then she looks at Liza, and she won't look at me, and she points her finger at Liza, which she's always telling me never to do because it's low class, and she says, "You tell America that I always liked him, before, and now, and forever, and I don't know where he got such trash from except it's false and the filthiest lie I ever heard in this life." Mrs. Harper puts her finger back into her hand, and sinks onto the pillow, and Liza opens her mouth to say something else, except Mrs. Harper sits up again quick, and points her finger out again straight at Liza and says, "And you tell America I love him."

"He's right here," Liza says. "You could tell him yourself."

But Mrs. Harper goes, "Good-bye now, Miss Liza," and then she shuts her eyes.

◆ ◆ ◆

We play baseball in the park. Browning can't find an official team, but we collect kids.

"Sure you can play," Browning goes loud, whenever anyone asks. "Anybody who wants can play." Enough kids start to join in that we have a game every afternoon. Browning refs and coaches.

"Unspring that coil," he calls out. "Eye on the ball, guys. Eye on the ball." He gives a dollar for every home run.

"Is he your father?" a kid asks.

"You got it," Browning answers for me.

"You don't look like his father," a couple of kids say.

"You don't look stupid," Browning tells them.

New kids ask all the time. "That dude is cool," they say. "Who is he?"

"He's my father," I tell them, proud. "But I call him Browning."

I like catching pop flys and pitches. In the outfield, I like the beat of my feet running to get underneath the ball, and the line of the ball as it drops out of the sky right to me, and the sound of the smack and the almost sting on my palm when it hits my glove. At the plate I like crouching behind my mask with Browning standing by me, coaching, and telling me I'm good, and pretending I'm his.

◆ ◆ ◆

"Listen," Browning says after he pours me my vodka and Coke. "We've got a couple of things to talk about."

"Okay," I say. "What?"

"We've got to take more pressure off Mrs. Harper."

"What pressure?" I ask. Mostly, she stays in her

room or watches TV on the couch. We do the shopping and cooking, and Browning helps her in the bath.

"We can't really talk about too much with her, you know?"

"Uh-uh."

"It's better if you just leave her be. It's better if you don't wear her out talking so much."

"I don't talk to her all that much," I say.

"Yes, you do," Browning says. "You and Liza get in there and wear poor Mrs. Harper to the bone. That's got to stop. You want to do right by her, don't you?"

"Yeah," I say. "But doesn't she need company, sometimes?"

"Yes and no," Browning says. "I keep telling you about old people. Mostly they like to be left alone."

—◆ ◆ ◆—

I don't want any pressure tiring her out too much, but still, when Browning's out, I think about when Mrs. Harper laughed with the letter and when she smiled at me remembering Clark Poignant, and I think of things to do in her room.

"You have certainly come a way," she says to me after I turn off the vacuum cleaner. Browning is out shopping. "No more of that foul mouth." She's all small from underneath one of her scarves. "Catching yourself up in school. Taking care of chores." She grabs my hand, and I stare at hers. It has way little patterns of way little lines curving over and over and over. Her skin looks like it would feel real rough and hard, like a lizard or alligator, only she's softer than anything I ever touched. She is so soft that every time her hand brushes mine, I'm surprised all over again.

"I'm blessed," she says, "to have two men taking such good care of me."

When she says that, touching my hand with her softness, it seems like the angels are lined up all over again downstairs, and Brooklyn and Lyle never happened, and I never got sent away. When she says that, I feel like a balloon, bright and floaty and full.

◆ ◆ ●

Liza's away at sleepover camp for the last month of the summer, and school's out. Browning starts the man kind of reading. It's another secret. Browning sets a vodka and Coke on the table next to my bed before we get started.

"What's that for?" I ask.

"A special treat," Browning says. He lights up a cigarette. "Sometimes a man likes a drink before bed."

I take a sip. It tastes more like vodka than like Coke. "It's strong," I say.

"My point exactly," Browning says. He squeezes in next to me and tosses a magazine in my lap. "No more kiddie reading," he says. "We're over that." He puts his arm around my shoulder and pulls the chain on the lamp next to my bed.

There's pictures of naked ladies all over the magazine, and some naked men, too. I think of Brooklyn and his TV channels, and I start to laugh.

"What's so funny?" Browning asks.

"This is dirty," I tell him.

"Now that's a shame," Browning says, inhaling. "It's not dirty. Who said it was dirty?"

"Liza," I tell him. "She showed me in the 7-Eleven."

"Well, Liza's got it all wrong," Browning says. "These are just pictures of people. And bodies. Nothing wrong with the naked body. You were born naked, weren't you?"

"I guess," I say. I take another sip of my vodka Coke.

"No guessing about it," Browning says. "Every single one of us was born naked. Liza included."

"Yeah, but it's sex," I tell Browning.

"Nothing wrong with sex, either," Browning says. "Sex is a beautiful thing. Now are you going to be a baby, or are you going to practice your reading?"

It's a story about a man who meets a woman at a party. The woman is pretty, and she has sex with a man while the first man watches, and then the first man has sex with the woman, and he likes it. I keep laughing while I'm reading because the story and words are funny and nasty and embarrassing, like the taste of your own breath first thing in the morning. It makes me laugh so much, I spill a little of my vodka Coke on my last gulp of it, and that gets Browning aggravated.

"Read regular," he tells me, crushing his cigarette on the side of my glass and smacking the side of my head. He hasn't smacked my head in a long time, so I put my glass on the floor and try to read regular, but it's hard. I can't help laughing.

Finally Browning pulls the magazine out of my hand. "I give up," he goes, all disappointed. "You're just too young for this." He takes a deep breath and lets it out in a big huff. "I was thinking you're getting to be a man, but maybe you're still just a kid." He sounds like he thinks I'm trying to be mean to him.

"Don't give up," I tell him. "I'm not too young."

He shakes his head. "Yeah." He sighs. "Nine years old. I guess you are."

"No, I'm not," I tell him.

"Maybe I'll just try to tutor someone else," Browning says. "Lots of kids in the park could use some help. But you. You've learned plenty. You don't really need me anymore."

"Yes, I do," I tell him. "I won't laugh. Come on, Browning, let me try one more time."

He sighs again, and thumbs through the magazine pages for a minute. "All right," he says. "If you really think you're ready."

— ● ● ● —

I drink my vodka and Coke every night in bed with Browning, and I get careful not to laugh. All the stories are sex stories, and I learn a lot of new words. Some of them are funny, and some of them aren't so funny and make me sweat. I'm always hot at night now, and I sleep real deep and long.

The problem is, during the day, I remember some of those stories, and it's real hard to get them out of my head. It's real hard not to picture what people do and how it feels, and it makes me get all warm, the way it is at night, reading the stories with Browning. Plus, it's real hard not to think a lot about Liza and how her body feels when she squeezes me. I try not to think about it, but I can't help it, and sometimes I touch myself the way the stories say people touch, and it feels just as good as in the stories, except sort of dirty, too, even though Browning says it isn't. I wish Liza were here and not at camp, so I could ask her about it, except Browning says the reading is a secret for males only, and I better not tell Liza, and if I do, he'll be so mad, he might never forgive me and he might never be able to speak to me again.

Plus, I wouldn't really know how to talk to Liza about it, anyway.

Now

Brooklyn's back. With that white apron and those see-through gloves, like all the other servers. And that scar. I watch him from the end of the line and let the other guys go ahead of me. I don't eat. I just keep my place at the end and watch him.

●●●

"You got another deck?"

"I do."

"Where?"

"It's somewhere in that basket."

"This?"

"That's it."

"Is this one missing any cards?"

"I don't think so. You can count them."

"You count them, B."

"Fifty-two."

"Cool. Give them here. We're going to play double-deck War."

"Hmm. Same rules?"

"What do you think, doc?"

"Anything special happen if we get a war between the two of spades?"

"Good question. What do you think?"

"I think probably."

"Well, you're right. Whoever wins a war between the two of spades wins the whole game right there."

"This is a switch from our last few sessions."

"Count your cards."

"You haven't been interested in playing for a while."

"Shut up with that, and throw down, man."

* * *

Now sometimes when we're playing, and I'm about to start floating with those flashes sliding through, I want to tell him some. Then I get scared. Then I get mad because I don't know what all I'm so scared of. Then I get more mad because he already knows I'm scared. Then I feel like a pussy and I hate my sorry-ass self.

Then I still want to tell him.

* * *

He won. He got all the aces and the two of spades straight up from the deal. I never even had a chance. "Can I go now?" I ask.

"You know we've got ten minutes left."

* * *

The truth of it is, those flashes happen everywhere. In the rec room watching Ping-Pong, in the cafeteria watching Brooklyn, in the main hall watching those skinny winter trees, in bed watching my feet, in session watching the cards. Your brain gets so damn weak some way, those flashes just keep coming, and you can't stop them.

●—●—●

I get to thinking about my file again. *America thought he was tough, but the truth is, America was a real punk for a long time. After a while, America got to be worse than a punk.* Liza said they knew things about you, even if you didn't tell them. *America got to be a pervert, and after that, he turned into a murderer.* I don't know how they get to know things, but if Liza's right, that shit could be right there in that file. *Stay away from America.*

●—●—●

We throw down and scoop up. Throw down and scoop up. It's real quiet. I'm quiet. He's quiet. I'm sick of the flashes. I'm sick of the quiet.

"You ever seen that **IMAX** on Everest?"

"The **IMAX**."

"It's high," I tell him.

"Hmm."

"It's all this snow and ice way up high. Higher than any other place in the whole damn world."

"Uh-huh."

"It's real beautiful."

"Really."

"It's real peaceful."

"Sounds like an important place."

I'm quiet, and it's boring.

"Our time's up," he tells me after a while. "I'll see you Tuesday."

"That's where I go," I tell him.

"Excuse me?"

"That's where I went that time," I say. "That time when I was here, but I wasn't here."

"Oh," he says.

●　●　●

I'm scared shitless. I'm afraid to sleep because of the dreams, and I'm afraid to be awake because all these flashes keep squeezing through and I can't stuff them back the way I used to. I'm afraid of never being able to get back up there to Everest, and I'm afraid that if I get back up there, I'll never come down, and I'm afraid of Dr. B. because he sees me and he knows things and when they see you and know things they mess everything up, and I'm afraid I'll be stuck in this place forever, and I'm afraid I won't, and I'm the biggest sorriest-ass pussy there ever was, and I'm just plain old fucking afraid.

●　●　●

I skip sessions and walk up and down the main hall looking through the windows at the ice all coating everything, trying to figure out how to get over to J building. Here's what one of the night nurses tells me. There's a courtyard and an entrance hall and then a long hallway and then another courtyard and then the front of J building. But you can't get far if you don't have the right pants. We wear green, and J building wears white. Man, Brooklyn must be pissed.

—●—●—●—

"What's been keeping you from coming to session?" Dr. B. asks.

"Nothing," I tell him.

"You've missed three in a row. A week and a half."

"Whatever," I say.

"What made you come back?" he goes.

"Nothing," I tell him.

"Something made you leave for a while, and something made you come back."

"Ah, man." He makes me tired.

"Thank you for telling me about your place," he says. "About Everest." My heart starts beating fast. I forgot I told him that. "I get the feeling you haven't shared that with anyone."

"So?"

"So. It must be something very personal and very important to you."

"Now I'm never getting out of here, right?" I go. "Because now you know I'm mental for real."

"You seem to think you're mental."

"I go up there, man," I tell him. "I'm there. I go there."

He nods. "Yes."

"Well, I'm right here," I tell him. "What are you? Stupid? How can I be there and here at the same time, if I'm not out of my tree?"

"I believe we've discussed this before. It's called

dissociation. It's a natural way to adapt to extremely difficult moments. Other people do it, too."

"Yeah, well, do other people like it?" I ask.

"Some people are afraid it means there's something wrong with their minds," he tells me. "But besides that, people seem to like it sometimes, and other times, they don't seem to."

"Oh," I go.

"How do *you* feel about it?"

I feel water filling up my eyes. The last time water came out, it didn't stop for so damn long. I make it go back in. "Whatever," I tell him.

And then we just sit there for a while.

Then

Dear Mrs. Harper,

I hope this letter finds you well.

I am writing to you today with some concern about America. Though he made significant progress in the previous two years, his social and academic performance at this time seems to be declining. According to his Individual Education Plan, which you may remember reviewing, we had hoped to mainstream America as he began sixth grade, next September. However, given his recent regression as the end of this school year approaches, we would now like to reevaluate.

I hope you will be able to make arrangements to meet with me so that we can discuss America further.

Thanks for your time, and I look forward to hearing from you soon.
Sincerely,
Mrs. Evans

— ◦ ◦ ◦ —

I flick my lighter and burn the letter over the sink. The fire alarm goes off as the flame crawls near my hand. I drop the letter, yank on the faucet full force, and then wave a dish towel at the ceiling to make the alarm stop.

"America!" Mrs. Harper yells from upstairs.

"It's burned toast!" I yell back. "Everything's cool!"

Browning's out again. I don't see him all that much during the day anymore. He stopped coaching baseball just before last Halloween, saying he got a job. I thought I'd start getting an allowance, like he promised, only he never brings any money home.

"What kind of job does he have, anyway?" Liza asks me. She got her hair cut short over Christmas vacation, and it makes her eyes look bigger.

"I don't know," I tell her.

"How can you not know?" Liza asks.

"Shut up," I say.

"You're so crabby," Liza says. She turns to Billy, which she does a lot more lately and which I hate. "Hey, Billy," she says. "Isn't America a pain in the ass?"

"Yeah," Billy says. I smack the side of his head.

"America!" Mrs. Evans goes. I watch her write another letter at her desk, from my time-out corner.

"You didn't have to hit him," Liza whispers to me. I don't answer her. She slides me a roll of Smarties, anyway.

"Thanks," I whisper.

She sniffs. "I don't even like Smarties," she says, but I know she's lying.

— • • —

We don't read stories too much anymore. Sometimes it starts out like that, but mostly Browning just begins by touching. At first, I believe him that it's cool, because it feels real nice. He talks to me soft, and his voice gets low, and he pats me all light, the way a father would take care of his baby, and it feels good. He tells me how what we're doing is a special secret, and how he wouldn't get with just anybody this way, and how he's helping me learn how to be a man, and how I'm such a good learner.

The nice part used to make me forget that it's dirty, but lately Browning's stopped talking to me. Lately, he gets quiet and goes far away while it's happening, and even though he looks at my face, he doesn't see me. Then it still feels good in my body, but it feels bad everywhere else, especially when after it's over, he starts snoring without getting into his own bed, and he's real heavy and makes my arm or my leg fall asleep, and he doesn't even say good night.

— • • —

Mrs. Harper is quieter than she used to be, and so am I. If I don't talk to her too much, I won't wear her out. So I just empty the trash or dust the TV.

"Thank you, America," she says a lot of times, and that makes me feel real ashamed.

Sometimes she'll scoot to the side of her bed and tell me to sit down. "How are things going?" she'll say.

"Fine," I'll say.

"You going to cook us dinner tonight?" she'll ask.

"Okay," I'll say.

"What will you make?"

"What do you want?"

"Oh, anything," she'll say. "Maybe some green beans and mashed potatoes. Chicken."

"You want garlic or sea salt tonight?" I'll ask.

"Garlic." She loves garlic. "You look tired," she'll say.

I never used to be tired.

"You want to watch TV with me before you start dinner?" she'll ask.

But I'm afraid if Browning finds out, he'll be mad, plus, what if he's right about old ladies and boys, and I end up killing her, just by wearing her out?

Or what if I can't help it, and I end up telling her about Browning and me, and she doesn't believe it? Or what if she does believe it, and she wonders why I don't make Browning stop, and then she figures out that my body even likes it, a little? What if she figures that out, and it makes her just keel over dead?

Dear Mrs. Harper,

I'm sorry to hear that you're not feeling well, and I regret having to trouble you, but it is imperative that we talk. America continues to regress socially and academically. He is fighting more with his peers, and is demonstrating a new difficulty following directions. He is also becoming increasingly oppositional toward me and the other teachers. It's very important that we discuss these issues at least by telephone so that we can address America's situation in the most constructive way possible.

Once again, thanks for your time, and I look forward to hearing from you soon.

Mrs. Evans

◆ ◆ ●

Now he makes me touch him. And other stuff. I tell him I don't want to, but he says you can't start a secret like we have and then stop it. He thinks it's important I learn about it with someone who cares. He's all how I'm ungrateful and selfish to tell him to stop. He tells me he knows I like it, so I may as well stop pretending.

I don't know too much else about it, though, because there's this thing you can do. You can make yourself fly up past the ceiling. You can make your-self stay up there, high and far away from everything. You can go right to Mount Everest, where the clouds and the snow look so much the same, you don't know where the clouds start or the snow ends. You can feel small and big and close and far all at the same time. You can feel dizzy and safe, both. You have to be careful not to look down and see what all's going on, because that's worse than anything and can make an avalanche crush you, but if you stay flying high looking up and out, you can freeze yourself and glide all the way through until the cold gets so cold, you just go numb all over, and it's like you're the last drip of an icicle that never got to drop but just froze instead. Every time you fly up high, past the ceiling all the way to Mount Everest, a little chip of yourself gets lost up there in all that cold, but you don't much care because it's better to lose a little piece of yourself than to let Browning find you and maybe make something dirty feel good.

• • •

Liza's trying to kiss me.

"Get off," I tell her.

"I hate you, America!" she says. We're cutting class, in the utility room. I bang my head against the cinder-block wall. It hurts, which feels good.

"Stop it," she goes. "Stop it!" I keep banging. My brain bounces. "Stop it!" Liza shouts.

"I'm going to kill myself," I tell her. Her face turns the color of sand, and she runs out of the utility room. I follow her, racing out of the building. She makes loud clopping noises because her soles are hard. I make squeaking noises because my soles are rubber. Mrs. Evans sees us. I hear her yelling for us to stop. Liza runs so fast, I can't keep up with her.

Three blocks away from the school I don't know where she is anymore. I walk back to class, and Mrs. Evans doesn't yell. She asks me what happened, and I tell her. Mrs. Evans takes me to the principal's office and calls Liza's mom. They talk for a long time. Then Mrs. Evans calls my number, but nobody answers. Browning is probably out, and Mrs. Harper's probably sleeping.

"Why do you want to kill yourself, America?" Mrs. Evans says.

"I don't," I tell her. "We were just kidding around."

"You've bruised your forehead," Mrs. Evans says. "That doesn't look like kidding around to me."

"It was a dare," I tell her. "Liza dared me to do it."

"Are you angry about something?" Mrs. Evans asks.

"No," I say.

"We need to get you some help," she says.

◆ ◆ ◆

"What should I paint?" I ask Liza. It's art, and she's making a killer whale out of clay. She loves whales. "Liza," I say. "What should I paint?"

"She's not talking to you," Billy says.

"Shut up," I tell him.

"You shut up," Liza says.

"I'll tell you a secret," I say. My chest goes thumpy.

"So?" Liza says.

"If you talk to me again, I'll tell it."

"I don't talk to people who are going to die," she says.

"Who's dying?" Billy says.

"Go away," Liza tells him.

"You're supposed to be my *friend*," he shrieks.

"Shut up," Liza says. Billy starts to try not to cry, but he can't. He throws his smock up over his face and sits down in the corner on the floor.

"He is so weird," Liza says.

"I'm not dying," I tell her.

"I hate people who kill themselves," she says. "So if you ever even try it, I will hate you and hate you and hate you like you never ever knew anybody could hate you."

"I won't kill myself," I say.

"I will hate you so bad," she says.

"I'm not going to," I say.

"Promise," she says. I don't want to promise. What if some time, the only way to get to Mount Everest is to die? "If you don't promise, I'm never speaking to you again, ever," Liza says.

"I promise," I say.

"What's the secret?" she asks.

My chest goes thumpier until I let myself know that I'm not for real going to tell. "Browning lets me drink vodka anytime I want now."

"That's not a secret," Liza goes. "America, sometimes you are so lame."

Then she squishes her killer whale and hugs me, and I try hard not to push her away, even though I'm afraid she'll smell Browning's smell on me, and she'll know, and she'll hate me forever, anyway.

• • •

The principal and Mrs. Evans like him a lot.

"Mrs. Harper sends her regards," Browning tells them while he's shaking their hands. "She's real sorry she can't make it, but you know. She's pretty frail and all."

He came home early last week and caught me about to burn another letter. He read it and then poured us each a drink.

"We'll take care of it," he told me. "We'll talk to them so we can all figure out how to fix it."

"I'm not trying to be bad," I told him.

"That's what I'm saying," he'd said. "You just *are* bad, and you can't help it." He'd poured more vodka into my Coke. "Me and your school people are going to try to help."

Now they ask me why.

"I don't know," I say.

"Is something bothering you?" Mrs. Evans asks.

"No," I answer.

"Are you upset about anything?"

"No," I say, but then I'm not sure.

"How is he at home?" the principal asks Browning.

"He's just fine," Browning says. "Does his chores, helps me and Mrs. Harper out. We've got no problems at home."

"Maybe you and I got on the wrong track some-how," Mrs. Evans says. "Do you think that might be it, America?"

104

"No," I tell her. "I'm just bad."

"You are not bad," Mrs. Evans says. But she doesn't know.

"We'd like to have America evaluated again," the principal says. "And we'd like to see if medication might be an option."

"I'm on board with whatever you need to do," Browning says. "Mrs. Harper will be, too."

"Is there anything at all you'd like to say or ask, America?" Mrs. Evans asks.

"No," I tell them.

After the meeting, Browning smokes three cigarettes in a row on the way to Friendly's. He buys me a banana split and lets me eat the whole thing without sharing. I save the cherry for Mrs. Harper, but it's smushed and covered with pocket dust when I get home, and when I poke my head into her room while Browning's setting the table, she's asleep.

"I see you," I whisper. "I see you." But she just snores a little and turns her head the other way.

* * *

I fly past the ceiling in school.

Liza kicks me, and it makes me fall back into my seat from Mount Everest. I'm mad because the sun shining on the snowflakes was bright and real beautiful, and I didn't want to leave it.

"America!" Mrs. Evans is saying, like she's been calling my name a million times.

"What!" I say.

"He spaced out again, Mrs. Evans," Liza says.

"I can see that, Liza," Mrs. Evans says. "Are you with us now, America?" she asks me.

"Uh-huh," I say.

• • •

"When they evaluate you, they find out stuff you never told them," Liza goes.

"How do they do that?" I ask her.

"They make you look at pictures and tell stories, and then they read your mind on what you really meant to say."

"You can't read people's minds," I tell her.

"They can," she says. "They read mine after my father left."

"Oh." I didn't know her father left.

"Yeah."

"What do you mean, he left?"

"Duh. He ditched me and my mom. Walked out and took all our money and never even said good-bye."

"Do you miss him?"

"I hate him," she says. "Stop talking about it."

"Was he cool?"

"I hate him, I told you," she says. "You can't be cool if you leave. He was cool, just as cool as Browning, but then he stopped being cool because he's an asshole because only assholes leave."

"Browning isn't so cool," I say.

"You're a moron," she says. "And you better not kill yourself."

"I won't," I say.

"You better not," she says. "Because killing yourself is just the same as leaving, only it's even worse than that."

"I wish I could, though."

"Why?" she asks, and then her eyes get watery.

"I don't know," I tell her. "Don't cry."

"What did I do?" She wipes her fist hard across her face.

"You didn't do anything," I tell her. "I'm only *not* doing it because of you."

"But why?"

"I don't know," I tell her. "I just don't like it here."

"You promised," she says.

"I know."

"You can't break promises."

"I know," I tell her.

"You better not."

"I won't," I say.

• • •

Browning knows about evaluations, too. He says I can't share any of our secrets during any evaluations. He says we have to take a nap before dinner. We never take naps.

"I'm not tired," I tell him.

"Yes, you are," he tells me.

We get into the bed, and I fly right up to Mount Everest. Only this time, something different happens. Something that yanks at me like a rope and pulls me hard, so I'm halfway up and halfway down, stuck, and it hurts. It hurts worse than anything. It hurts worse than Brooklyn and Lyle and the people beating you down all at the same time. It hurts as much as Liza said she would hate me if I kill myself. It hurts, and it won't let me fly up. It pulls me down below with him, and it hurts.

●━●━●

Browning doesn't fall asleep after.

"We should get dinner going," he says, pulling up his pants.

When I walk into the kitchen a little while later, he's sitting at the table. He has a pile of carrots and a metal mixing bowl in front of him. He has a carrot scraper in his hand. He points to the chair across from him for me to sit in, so I do. It hurts.

"We've got a lot of carrots to scrape tonight," Browning tells me. "Watch how I do it."

"I know how to scrape carrots," I tell him.

"Uh-huh," Browning says. Then he starts to scrape. He scrapes the peels into the bowl.

"Imagine," he tells me after the first carrot. "If this was someone's finger?" I hurt a lot. "Could you imagine," he says, "what it would feel like to have your finger scraped? To peel the skin of your finger right off?" He doesn't wait for me to answer, and he doesn't look at me. He's just staring at his scraper and his carrot. "Imagine what it would feel like to have every single finger on both hands scraped. Just like a carrot."

"It would hurt," I say.

He nods. "My point exactly," he says. He scrapes a few more carrots, and I watch, because I'm too tired to do anything else. After awhile, he says,

"Could you imagine what it would be like to have all your fingers scraped, and then to watch someone else getting their fingers scraped?" I wish I hadn't promised Liza. "Could you imagine, say, if that someone else was somebody you really liked a whole lot?" He's quiet again for a whole other carrot. He scrapes it extra slow. "Like, say, Mrs. Harper? You should try to imagine it, America." He sighs and then starts to hum. Those scraped carrots are bright, lined up next to each other on the table near the shiny bowl full of their skins. Those carrots are bright and wet looking. "You should just try to imagine it." Browning says. "As a way to think about what things might be like, if you ever told our secrets."

And now, me and him and Mrs. Harper are eating those carrots in a salad and waiting for the spaghetti to be done, and I'm watching us from a real, real high place. So high and so cold and so sparkly that it's nicer than it's ever been before, and nothing hurts.

* * *

When I come down from the cold in the middle of the night, the light in the hall is burned out so I feel my way to Mrs. Harper's room. I hear her snoring, and I stand in front of her for a long time, letting my eyes get used to the darkness. Then I touch her soft, soft hand and the smooth top of her round, black ring.

I know I'll need money, and I know Mrs. Harper keeps her cash in the bottom drawer. So I look, real quiet, until I find her piles of bills, stacked tight with rubber bands, and then I tiptoe into the bathroom to count it all. At the bottom of the third pile, folded up longwise, there's some piece of paper. Some chart, or something.

GRACIE HOUSE DRUG AND ALCOHOL REHAB.

Exercise Five

ME	MY BABIES	DRUG MONEY	MATH
Fifteen years old	Jade	$25 a week	$25 times 52
Sixteen years old	Pearl	$50 a week	$50 times 52
Seventeen years old	Kyle, Lyle	$100 a week	$100 times 52
Legal	Brooklyn	$200 a week	$200 times 52
Nineteen years old	America	$40 a day	$40 times 365
Total		Could have bought me a damn house	

For a second I try to remember the lady who was my mother, but I can't. And even though I know she's the one who must have written up this chart, I'm too tired to figure out what it means or how Mrs. Harper got it, and it's too much to care about, anyway, so I try to fly up high, but I can't do that, either, so instead I hold the paper over the sink and pull out my lighter and watch it burn. There's no smoke alarm up here to bother with, only in the kitchen and at the foot of the stairs, and the yellow and blue of the flames look real nice against their own black burn line, and I look at them awhile. I still hurt, and I want to say good-bye to Liza, but if I call her house everyone will know, so I don't. I go into my room and throw the ashes of my mother's chart onto Browning, only they don't throw so good. They flutter instead, which makes me mad. So then I sit on the edge of my bed and watch my lighter burn for a long time.

"Go to sleep, America," Browning mutters, so I snap the lighter closed. Then I pull on my jeans and a shirt and stuff Mrs. Harper's money in my back pocket, and just before I walk out of the room, I get the idea, and it seems like the right thing. So I hold up the end of Browning's blanket at the foot of his bed, and I flick on my lighter again. The blanket catches fast, with little flames at first, dancing all along the blanket's edge like overgrown grass blades against the fence bottom on a real windy day. I watch the little flames grow longer and wider and peel off into new flames, and then I go downstairs and find my shoes, and I tie them so quick that by the time I'm a few blocks away from Mrs. Harper's house, one of them's untied and all pulled undone, and it's raggedy at the tip, and I know I'm never going to be able to string it back through.

Now

You're all set to die, and then things happen that make you need some shit before you check out. Some shit you can't even explain to your own self, and needing it messes up all your plans.

⎯•⎯•⎯•⎯

"Saw a guy in green pants in the back of the kitchen," I say.

"Did you?" Dr. B. goes.

"Yeah," I say. "What's up with that?"

"What do you mean, what's up with that?"

"You said only J building guys get to be in the kitchen."

"No, I said only J building guys serve."

"You mean, other guys get to do the food?"

"Other guys who've achieved a certain level of stability and who want to. Yes."

"What level of stability?"

"They can't be suicidal, for one," Dr. B. says. "Because of the access to knives, among other things."

"Oh," I go.

"You'd like to work in the kitchen."

"Maybe," I go.

"In order to work in the kitchen, you can't be feeling a desire to be dead."

"Whatever," I go.

"What is it about the kitchen that makes you want to work there?"

"Bored," I tell him.

"When we're bored, there's usually some other feelings underneath the boredom."

"You got that right: more boredom."

"You could participate in sports. There's arts and crafts. Schoolwork. Game room. Group. Psychodrama. Grounds work. There are lots of ways to alleviate boredom here."

"So?"

"So I'm interested in why you're particularly pursuing kitchen work when you've been less than thrilled with other activities."

"Food here sucks," I tell him. "Just because I'm crazy doesn't mean I have to eat shit."

"Hmm," Dr. B. says.

●－●－●

I stand in the back of the line, and I watch him. Some kid starts bitching.

"That's hardly any," this dude goes when Brooklyn dumps rice on his plate. "Give me a little more, man. Damn." Brooklyn stares at him a second and then takes the plate. He spits in the kid's rice and hands that shit right back over. That's Brooklyn. Still badder than anybody.

— • • • —

"I have something to tell you," Dr. B. goes.

"What?"

"I'll be going away for two weeks in March."

"So?"

"We'll miss two weeks of session, and then I'll be back, and we'll continue as usual."

"So?"

"We have four weeks prior to the two weeks we'll skip."

"So?"

"Another doctor will be covering for me while I'm gone, if you want to speak to anyone during that time."

"So?"

"Do you have any questions about this, or anything you'd like to say?"

"Yeah. Cut the damn deck so I can deal here."

— • • • —

They're talking some shit in group, but I'm doing my own thing. I'm thinking a little, just for the hell of it. I'm thinking, that's how it goes. Nobody sticks around for long. Nobody can stand you for long. *America's mother left him twice.* My file probably says it clear as anything. *America's mother left him to run all kinds of errands and take all kinds of drugs and have sex with all kinds of men.* Those files tell it like it is. People are all the time pretending they care, but the truth is, they can't wait until their stupid errands. Stupid vacations. Once they get out of here, they never come back.

• • •

Ping. Pong. Ping. Pong.

How do you know if you really want to be dead? You have those times when you feel so bad, the shame makes your skin feel inside out and that's when you know you ought to be dead even if you deep down inside don't want to die. You have those times. But other times you want to say something to Brooklyn. Or you want to visit Mrs. Harper and tell her you didn't mean it. Or you want to see Liza again. Or you want to figure out some way not to let Dr. B. just up and go like that because even if it is pussy, you went ahead and ended up real used to him.

So then you get stuck. You make yourself in the middle place. This place where you don't think shit, you don't feel shit, you don't know shit. You just do. You're like some zombie or some junkie where you can't hardly even stand up, but somehow you don't fall down, either. You're just there. Nothing.

Then

I see myself in a mall. I watch myself crying. There's no part of me that cares one way or the other about it.

I see myself cry and watch the televisions. They're in a pyramid, all on the same channel. The sound is off most of the time, but I can tell that Browning died. I can tell from the way they show the paramedics carrying out a stretcher with a plastic blanket over it, and no head sticking out. I can't tell what happened to Mrs. Harper. They don't show her on a stretcher or anywhere. The picture of me is the one from over the fireplace. It doesn't look like me. It looks like a little kid. They show it a lot at first.

* * *

I cry so much, I don't even notice it anymore. I cry so much, things are blurry all the time, on the outside and on the inside. I cry hiding in the fountain until the security guards pass by every night. I cry by the McDonald's garbage while I dig for fries. I cry under the display beds in Sears. I cry while I'm peeing, and I cry playing video games in the arcade. I stare up at the security cameras and cry and cry, and nobody notices me. You can be disappeared anywhere, if you're bad enough.

— • • •

"Hey," I see myself say.

The little girl looks up. "What?" the little girl says.

"Can I have those?"

"I need them." Her shoelaces look real new, and they've got dinosaurs on them.

"Can I have them?" I ask.

"Why are you crying?" she says.

"Can I have them?"

"My mom will get mad," she tells me.

I find the Hallmark where they have the dinosaur shoelaces, plus heart shoelaces, laces with fish on them, striped shoelaces, and shoelaces with candy canes on them. They also have black, yellow, red, purple, and brown shoelaces. I need them all.

— • • •

A man catches me wrapping my fingers around three pairs of brown, and he brings me to a room near The Sports Authority. "You wait here," he says.

Then he turns his back on me and walks out. I see myself follow him so quiet, he doesn't know I'm there. Then I see myself run down the up escalator and outside into the parking lot. The light makes my eyes squint, but I don't feel the hurt. I walk a long time, and then I get on a train. It goes to New York City, where you can be disappeared. Where Brooklyn and Lyle were. I watch myself cry on the train.

◆ ◆ ◆

I sleep in the park. There are three different places where you can crawl into bushes, and nobody knows you're there. There are four places where you can crawl and other people are there, but nobody cares and they don't bother you. You can drink from the water fountains and get clean, too. Sort of. You can live off hot dogs and soda and pretzels and ice cream. If your money runs out, you can ask for some or find some on the ground or steal.

You can walk all around the city and see things. Double-decker tour buses. Taxis and black limos. Revolving doors. People who are lost and trying to be found with signs saying that they're homeless or sick and to please give them money. You can see eight or ten dogs all being walked by one person. You can see a man who paints himself silver and stands on a bucket so still, he looks like a statue. He only moves after someone puts change in another bucket at his feet. You can see people playing musical instruments right on the sidewalk. You can see them everywhere selling perfume and clothes and sunglasses and watches. And shoelaces. You can see men on bikes wearing tight black shorts and helmets with bags full of packages slung over their chests. You can walk and walk and walk, just like everybody else.

The park is for when you're tired of walking. I watch myself watching the skaters. The kids with knee pads and helmets who trick-skate on the benches and down steps skate right through me. But the grown people who dance-skate in a circle sometimes nod or stay fallen down for a while near to where I'm sitting, in the grass or on a bench.

"Keep this for me, and I'll give you five bucks," this one man says after a lot of weeks of me sitting and watching and crying. I watch myself say okay and then shove his knapsack between my knees. When he comes back, he gives me five dollars and drops himself next to me. His skates are the old-fashioned kind, not the Rollerblade kind. They're black and scuffed. I've seen him a lot, but never without those skates on. He's one of the best dance-skaters in the park.

"Still crying, huh?" he says.

"So?" I say.

A lady with orange shoes comes up to us and hands him some money. I don't see how much. She's been around before.

"What's up, Ty?" she goes, and he digs into his knapsack and pulls out a plastic Baggie filled with some mess.

"What's up?" he says, and she takes it and leaves. "You're not a narc, are you?" he asks me. Then he laughs.

I watch him laugh while I cry, and the skaters in front of us show off for the tourists who take pictures. They never stop moving, the skaters. Everybody crowds together to look at them, like they're a movie or a circus, and the crowd of lookers always ends up jiggling and bumping in time with the skaters and their music.

"It'll be cold, soon," Ty says.

"So?" I say.

"So where are you going to sleep?"

Two guys with their shirts off come over and shake his hand. I've seen them before, too. They hand him their money. "That your new date?" they ask him, nodding at me. "This one doesn't look too happy, man."

Ty gives them their Baggies and doesn't answer. "What's your name?" he asks me after they're gone.

"America," I hear myself say.

"Beautiful," he says. "You watch my bag while I skate, and you can crash with me when it gets cold."

"Don't touch me," I tell him.

"Don't worry," he says. Then he gets up to dance.

◆ ◆ ◆

I watch myself sleep at Ty's place. His couch is soft and clean. Ty lets me keep my things underneath the couch in a plastic grocery store bag. My things are all my shoelaces. Ty never touches me. He doesn't have a TV. He reads in his bed in the other room. He hides his books under his bed. Sometimes he has sex in there with his friends.

"Why's he always crying?" the one with all the earrings says every time she's over.

"What the hell are you doing to that kid?" another one asks.

I watch myself lie on the couch, hearing them or hearing Ty read. He'll leave his door open sometimes when there's no females around, and he'll read out loud. The first time, I start to fly up to Everest, but then I come back down because it's this story about some girl way back a real long time ago when there were Indians and houses made out of mud and logs.

"You tell anyone I read Laura Ingalls, and you're never crashing here again," Ty tells me.

I watch myself cry and cry and cry.

—◆ ◆ ◆—

There's not as many people in the park because it's colder. But Ty still skates and sells every day. I watch his bag and cry every day. I watch us sit on the grass a lot and not talk. Sometimes he skates away and doesn't come back until dark. I don't walk anymore. I stay with the bag. I watch myself living like that for a long time.

"You must have some kind of record, or something," Ty says one day after he's skated back to the grass with a new blue bubble coat for me.

"So?" I say. I watch myself take the coat and pull it into my lap.

"Doesn't your head hurt, or your eyes, man? They're always red as hell."

"Nothing hurts."

"So why are you crying?" he goes.

"I'm not crying," I see myself tell him.

"You're some weird kid," he says.

◆ ◆ ◆

Mostly what Ty reads is boring, and I lose track of the story. But I keep hearing his voice. His voice is like a light in the blur that is me. When the words fade away, the light is still there. I fall asleep with the light of his voice a lot of times, over and over and over, and then one day, I see myself wake up, and I'm not crying.

◆ ◆ ◆

I don't feel anything, but it must be cold because there's snow and ice, and Ty makes me pull the hood of the bubble coat tight on my head. Now he only sells four days a week. I have to stand outside in the empty park with the knapsack while he skates his rounds.

I stand or sit on the frozen grass for a lot of hours at a time. I see myself do it, and it's like a movie of nothing with the sound off. I watch myself stay in the middle of the grass in the middle of the park in the middle of New York City in the middle of New York State on the edge of America. I am in America and America is me.

It's not blurry anymore. It's real clear. It's quiet.

◆ ◆ ◆

I watch myself asleep on the couch when there's a knock at the door.

"Shit," I hear Ty say, and then I hear the one with all the earrings go, "What?" There's another knock, and it's louder, and the earring girl goes, "Who the hell is that?"

"Shit," Ty says again. I watch him walk out of his bedroom and stand at the foot of the couch looking at me. "Man," he says.

"Who is it?" I watch myself ask him.

"Charles Tyler, open the door," they say from outside.

"Don't tell me this is a bust," the earring girl says.

"NYPD," they say. "Open the door now, or we'll open it for you."

"Shit," Ty says, and lets them in.

"How you doing, Ty?" the first cop says.

Ty crosses his arms and doesn't move away from the door. "What is this?" he says.

"What do you think?" the cop says. The other cop pushes past Ty and starts to poke around in the front closet.

"Who's the kid?" the second cop says.

"My nephew," Ty says.

"I'm getting out of here," the earring girl says. She's got her clothes on now, and she pushes past Ty, too. The cops don't stop her.

"Another nephew?" the cop says.

"Christ," Ty says.

"Does this guy touch you?" the cop asks me.

Ty looks at me. "Get out of here, man," he says.

I watch myself not move. Mrs. Harper said if you need help, you can go to a policeman.

"He your uncle?" the first cop says.

"Nuh-uh," I see myself say.

"He touch you?" the cop says.

"Nuh-uh." Every time Brooklyn saw policemen, he hid real quick.

"You see him dealing?" the cop says.

"Nuh-uh." Brooklyn said they'll beat you worse than anyone. He said they'll kill you.

They put handcuffs on Ty.

"Keep the coat, man," he tells me. I watch myself pull my plastic grocery store bag out from underneath the couch. The first cop snatches it and dumps the shoelaces onto the floor. There's only five pairs left. I'm running out.

"Christ," the cop says.

Ty snorts while I pick my stuff back up. "That's some serious dope, huh?" he smart mouths to the cop.

"Shut up," the cop says.

I watch them put Ty in their car, and then I watch all of us waiting for some other car to come and pick me up.

· * * ·

Another office. Another chair. Blue carpet on the floor. A gray metal desk. A one-way mirror with the mirror side facing us. I watch myself answer questions.

"Nyack's a ways away," the detective says. A phone. I watch myself pick up a pen and write my numbers on a long yellow pad with blue lines. I watch the cop watching.

"How long you been staying with Ty," the detective says.

"Don't know," I watch myself say.

124

"Couple of months?" the cop asks. "Couple of years?"

"Don't know," I say.

"You sure he never touched you?"

"Uh-huh."

The detective pulls out a pack of gum from his back pocket. "You want some?"

I watch myself shake my head. He drags out a pack of cigarettes and a lighter. He holds out the cigarettes. I watch myself ignore the cigarettes and take the lighter instead. I watch him watching me light the lighter and stare at the flame.

"So why'd you leave Nyack?" the cop says.

"Had to." I used to like the yellow of the flame with the blue at the bottom. I used to stare at it. Now it's nothing. I don't like it. I don't not like it. But I have to stare at it.

"Your parents looking for you?" the detective asks.

"Nah," I say.

"Anyone looking for you?" the detective says.

"Maybe the cops," I hear myself tell him.

"Oh, yeah?" the detective says. "That why you left?"

"Yeah," I say. I turn the wheel of the lighter to make the flame as high as it will go. I used to like the way the yellow and blue met in a little black line if you look at it just right.

"What'd you do?" the detective asks.

"Killed somebody," I watch myself tell him.

"You what?"

"Killed this man," I tell him.

"Are you shitting me?" the detective asks.

I watch myself look up from the flame. "Nah."

❖ ❖ ❖

There's five other guys in the van besides me. Three black, one white, and one Puerto Rican.

"Freak," one of the black ones says to me.

"He's Cambodian, or some shit," the Puerto Rican says.

"Are you Cambodian?" the white one says. I don't answer.

"What'd you do?" the second black one says.

"Weed, probably," the first one says.

"You sold weed?" the Puerto Rican says. "You going to jail for weed?"

"It ain't jail, man," the third black one goes. "It's R and D."

"What's R and D?" the white one says.

"Reception and Diagnostic."

"Reception and what?"

"They receive your ass, diagnose your ass, and then send your ass to do its time."

"How much time is he going to do for weed?" the white one asks.

"You sold weed?" the Puerto Rican goes. "That's all you did? Sold some weed?"

"Nah," I watch myself say.

"Y'all better leave that one alone," the guard in the backseat calls out. He's leaning the side of his head against the window.

"What'd he do?" the first black one asks. "Unload some fake Louis?" He cracks up.

"Says he killed a guy," the guard goes, closing his eyes. "Burned a guy up."

"You fried a guy?" the white kid goes.

I watch myself shrug. They leave me alone after that for a long time.

A long time. A lot of days. A lot of weeks. A lot of months. It gets hot again, but there's no skaters. They leave me alone. Then it gets cold again, but there's no blue bubble coat. Then it gets green again. They still leave me alone. A long time. A real long time.

• • •

I watch myself watching them argue. It's a social worker, a lawyer for me, a lawyer against me, a cop, a judge, and some people.

"We've located a missing person matching this boy's information," the social worker says, "but there's no warrant involved."

"However, Your Honor," the lawyer against me says, "there is record of a death by fire."

"The guardian reports the boy disappeared a full eighteen hours prior to said fire," the lawyer for me says. "In addition to which, the fire was cleared of arson and declared an accident. Smoking-in-bed situation."

"The kid can't keep his hands off lighters, Your Honor," the lawyer against me says. "Not to mention that the kid confessed, here."

"Is the boy wanted for a crime in Nyack or not?" the judge asks.

"He is not, Your Honor," the lawyer for me says.

"However, it would be prudent to reexamine the case, given the boy's recent confession," the lawyer against me says.

"You're repeating yourself, McKinsey," the judge tells him. "I heard you the first time." Then he looks at the cop. "Is family of the deceased asking for a reopening?"

"No, Your Honor," the cop says.

"Is the guardian asking for a reopening?"

"No, Your Honor," the cop says.

"Is Nyack asking for a reopening?"

"No, sir."

"Where is the guardian?" the judge asks.

"She's unable to care for the boy, Your Honor," the social worker says. "But she's expressed the desire for him to return. She expresses a strong attachment to the boy."

"I believe I asked where she is," the judge says.

"In a nursing home, Your Honor," the social worker answers. "In Nyack."

"The guardian is in Nyack?" the judge says. His voice gets louder. "How long was this boy detained at R and D?" I see the quiet and the way the judge's face turns red. "Why is this boy in Manhattan?" Nobody answers. "Why is this boy in front of me?" Nobody answers. "Anyone?" the judge says.

"I got lost in the system," I watch myself say.

"Jesus Christ," the judge says.

Now

"I want to remind you that next Thursday will be the last session before our two-week break."

"I want to work in the kitchen."

"Hmm."

"I want to cook."

"Did you hear what I said, America?"

"Yeah, I heard you. You think I'm deaf or something?"

"You didn't respond."

"Because I don't give a shit about your stupid vacation."

"Hmm."

"I'm trying to talk about the kitchen, here."

"Okay."

"I'm a good cook."

"Really? How did you learn?"

"Huh?"

"How did you learn how to cook?"

"Time up yet?"

"You know we just started, America."

"Boring."

"Something about how you learned to cook is boring?"

"Ah, man."

"You're having feelings."

"That's right, man. I'm feeling that I hate you."

"You're angry."

"I'm not angry, man. I just hate you."

"And you're scared."

"I hate you."

"Something about my vacation, or learning to cook, or maybe both makes you angry and scared."

"I hate you."

•—•—•

"Brooklyn," I go. His head whips up. "Brooklyn," I go again. He wipes his eye with the back of his hand. "You're dripping beans, man," I go.

He looks at the mess on the counter. He puts down his spoon and peels off his gloves. "Break," he yells, and walks away, banging through those swinging doors back there.

•—•—•

"This Thursday will be our final session before the two-week break." I hang my head way back and check out those sand soldiers.

"What two-week break?" They fill up five whole shelves. Shooting and running and drumming and kicking and all kinds of fighting shit.

"Remember? I'm leaving for two weeks. We'll miss four sessions. Another doctor will cover for me while I'm gone if you want to speak with someone about anything. Then I'll be back, and we'll continue as usual."

"Since when?" I sit up.

"Since when, what?"

"Since when are you going away?"

"I first told you a month ago, America. And I've mentioned it periodically since then."

"Bullshit."

"I reminded you during our last session."

"No, you didn't."

"Hmm."

"When are you coming back?"

"Two weeks."

"So I don't have to see your ass for two weeks?"

"That's right."

"Cool."

* * *

I sit in group and get curious.

About my mother. I bet there's a mess of stuff on her in my file. *America's mother was a real easy woman. Plus, America's mother was proud she had sex with so many different kinds of people. By the time America's mother gave birth to America, she knew his father could be just about any man in the entire country. She knew America might look like just about any kind of man she ever met. That's how America's mother thought up the name America.*

I lie in my bed, and I get to wondering.

About Brooklyn. About what he's on and how he got on it. Like if he drinks, or if he's some kid crackhead. Like if he got arrested anytime, and if he gets flashes when he's high. Or does drinking a whole lot of beers or Jim Beam, or something, keep his flashes all sealed out?

"You ever mess with alcohol?"

"What makes you ask?"

"Did you?"

"What do you imagine?"

"You always ask me that, man."

"You sound aggravated."

"You got that right."

"What makes you aggravated?"

"You're like a dog with a bone, man."

"Meaning?"

"You never give up. You just ask and ask and ask and it's never enough. You keep worrying it. You never let anything go."

"Do you want me to give up?"

I'm up here. It's cold and white. I'm all alone, and it's safe.

"America!"

Go away.

"America!"

"What!"

"You went there, didn't you?"

"The hell are you talking about, man?"

"Everest. Did you go there?"

"Nah."

"You don't have to lie to me."

"Nah."

"Something frightened you and you went there."

"Nah."

"Something that happened between us."

The water gets in my eyes.

"Something happened between us that frightened you."

"Nah."

"Yes."

"Nah."

"I'll be back in two weeks. And I'm not giving up."

"Huh?"

"I'll be back in two weeks. And I'm not giving up."

"Nah."

Then

I'm on some train. Going north. It's hotter than anything. It's not buildings out the windows anymore. It's just trees.

"What's the matter with the old ones?" the escort asks me. I don't answer him. I just watch myself keep on restringing my shoelaces. "Applegate isn't so bad," the escort says. His face is all shiny with sweat. "Counselors are pretty good. Food could be worse. You get cable. You get trips."

◆ ◆ ◆

I see myself in Cottage Four.

"Say hi to America," the counselor says.

"You touch my bed, my shelf, my sink, or my hook, and I'll rearrange your face," a tall white kid tells me.

"You want points this evening, Wick?" the counselor asks.

I watch myself make up a bed. I watch myself put

the bag on a shelf. I watch myself hang the next pair of shoelaces on a hook.

"What's his name, Tom?" another kid asks the counselor. He's got two oval tattoos over his eyebrows. He's white, too. They're all white.

"America," Tom says. He looks at me. "That's Marshall." He points to the tattoo kid. Then he points to another kid who's got drool on his chin. "That's Fish."

"Fish isn't supposed to be here," Marshall says. "His brain's up his butt."

"Enough, Marshall," Tom says. He points again. "That's Ernie."

Ernie's got one blue eye and one brown eye. The glasses he wears make them look real big.

"No points," Ernie says when I light my lighter.

"Where did you get that?" Tom says. He holds out his hand. "No lighters allowed, America. Sorry." I watch myself give it up.

"Looks like we got a good boy," Marshall says. His eyebrows go up, and his oval tattoos turn into straight lines.

"So where's he from?" Wick asks Tom.

"Ask him yourself," Tom says.

"Where are you from?" Wick asks me. I watch myself not answer. "I said," Wick says, "where are you from?"

"Nowhere," I say.

"Ah, fuck," Wick says.

"Points," Tom says to Wick.

"Fuck points," Marshall says.

"Fuck points," Fish says.

"What have I told you?" Tom says to Wick and Marshall. Then he goes to Fish, "Don't say that word, Fish. That's a bad word."

"Fuck points?" Fish says. Then he picks up my hand. I watch myself let him hold it.

— • —

"You don't usually get girls," Ernie tells me on the way to class. "That's why Apple's better than other places. Cottage Eight and us have all our classes with GC 4 and GC 8. That means Girls' Cottage Four and Girls' Cottage Eight. Get it? Nobody told me when I got here, and it took me, like, weeks to figure it out."

"You're America?" a lady teacher says when we walk into the classroom.

Ernie keeps talking. "We get dances one time a month with them. It costs five tickets."

"Welcome, America. Now please go to room four hundred," the teacher says.

"They'll tell you after testing, but ten points earns a ticket. So you need, like, fifty points to go to a dance. But you can earn thirty points a day, so it's not a big deal, unless you're like those guys." He jerks his head toward Wick and Marshall.

"Down the hall and to your right," the teacher says.

"Answer 'B' for all the multiple choice," Wick tells me. He doesn't keep his voice down, the way Ernie does.

"I don't believe America asked you for your input, Wick," the teacher says.

136

"If you answer all 'B' you get two million points," Wick says. "You can trade them for a million tickets, and a million tickets buy you independent minor status and your own car." He laughs hard and slams his fist on the table.

I watch myself leave the room.

• • •

It's not school tests yet. It's evaluation tests. The kind Liza said they can read your mind on. The lady holds up cards with spilled paint on them and asks me what they look like. I tell her *nothing* every time. The lady shows me little kid pictures and asks me to tell a story about them. I watch myself stay quiet.

"What's happening here, do you think?" the lady asks. The picture is of a man and a dog.

"Nothing," I say.

She holds up another picture. "Let's try this one," she says. It's got two boys on it. One of them has a ball. Another one has a pocketknife.

"B," I hear myself say.

"Excuse me?" she says.

"Nothing."

She shows me shapes, and tells me to draw them the same way on another piece of paper. I draw them exactly the same way. She gives me puzzles and tells me to put them together. I watch myself do it. I watch her write things down on a clipboard.

"Let's try the cards again," she says. She holds up one of the first cards with the spilled paint. "So what does this look like to you?" she says.

"Nothing," I tell her.

"You sure?" she says.

"Nothing," I see myself say.

— • • •

I see her four more times every morning for the rest of the week. Plus, I earn 150 points.

"You have enough for more than ten tickets," Marshall tells me. Everyone knows how many points everyone else has. Everyone knows how many tickets that makes. I have the most. Wick has the least. "More than ten tickets," Marshall says again.

"Whatever," I say.

"You've got to trade them in for privileges," Marshall says. "You get a half day out with ten tickets." I watch myself shrug. "He hasn't traded his points in," Marshall says to Wick.

"You've got to trade them in," Wick says. "Points only get you tickets. Tickets get you the good stuff."

"Whatever," I hear myself say.

"If you're not using them, give them to me," Marshall says.

"Nah," I say.

"I'll buy them off you," Marshall goes.

"He wants to see Shiri," Ernie says.

"I'm buying them," Wick tells Marshall. "What do you want?" he asks me.

"Nothing," I say.

"There's got to be something," Wick says. "What do you want?"

"A pair of shoelaces for ten points," I see myself tell him.

138

"This guy is sick," Marshall says.

"You can't transfer points," Ernie says.

"Shut up," Marshall and Wick say at the same time.

But Ernie's right. You can't.

◆ ◆ ◆

"I'm Mr. Patterson," the man says. He points to one of the gray armchairs. Its seat is worn to a whole shade lighter than the rest of it. "I'm your therapist." I watch myself sit. "I hear you don't talk much," he says. I shrug. "I wonder why?" I see myself stare past him out the window. "I hear you're not interested in tickets," he says. I shrug again. "You don't want to go to the mall?" he asks. I watch myself not answer. "You don't want your allowance?" Shoelaces. My last pair are about to get raggedy at the tip.

"You get allowance with tickets?" I hear myself ask.

Mr. Patterson smiles. "You can trade ten tickets for three dollars," he says. "Ernie didn't tell you?"

"Nah," I say. "So who do I get my tickets from?"

"You get them from your cottage counselor. I believe in your case that would be Tom."

"Okay," I say.

"Excellent," Mr. Patterson says. "Now I wonder what you can tell me about yourself." I watch myself not answer. "I'm told you haven't put anyone on your visitors list." He waits a second, and then he says, "I wonder why."

There's a field and then a fence out the window. But the fence is so far away, you almost can't see it. The field is big. There's a tree right in the middle of it. The tree's big, too.

"What about your Mrs. Hopper?" He picks up some folder from off his desk. He looks at it, turning all kinds of pages. "Mrs. Harper. I believe she raised you?"

"Whatever," I say.

He puts the folder down. "I wonder how you feel about the idea of seeing her?" He drums his fingers on his desk. A lot of seconds pass. He picks up the folder again and opens it. "You were on your own for a long time," he says, reading something in there. "I wonder what that was like for you." I watch myself bend down and restring my laces. I watch myself string them backward. "Before you were on your own, I believe there was a man who died," Mr. Patterson says after a while. He squints at the folder. "A man who also raised you." I straighten up and stretch my legs out and look at the laces. "I wonder how you feel about that," Mr. Patterson says. "I understand you mentioned some things about his death." His fingers get ready to drum on the desk again. "I wonder what some of your thoughts and feelings are about him." I watch myself not answer. Mr. Patterson gets quiet again, but not for too long. "I wonder how you're feeling right now. Here, in this room." I watch myself cross my arms and turn my head to the window.

Mr. Patterson wonders about a lot more things, and I stare out at the field.

◆ ◆ ◆

They don't tell you what grade level you test at. All the C4s and C8s are in the same classroom, anyway. Even Fish.

"What have you read lately?" the teacher asks me.

"Nothing," I hear myself say. Wick snorts.

"Wick," the teacher says. "What is the last book you've read?"

"Huh?" Wick says.

"I gave you a list of titles last month," the teacher says. "So which one did you read?"

"The dog ate it," Wick says, and he and Marshall and Shiri crack up.

• • •

On visiting day, I watch myself go to the mall with Ernie.

"Be at the elevator banks at four o'clock sharp," Tom says.

"Normally, Wick and Marshall would be pissed they can't go," Ernie says. "But Shiri's on punishment, so she can't go out, so they don't care." I watch myself not talk to him. "Where do you want to go first?" He follows me. "They've got some great games on the third floor," he says. "And thick-crust pizza over there, behind the frozen yogurt place." I just keep walking. "You can make your own CD," Ernie says. "They have this booth next to Radio-Shack."

I find a Hallmark, but there's no shoelaces. I check every aisle. There's only cards. "Is there a shoe store in this place?" I ask Ernie.

I buy five pairs of black and five pairs of white. Ernie finally shuts up when I'm paying. He doesn't say one word.

• • •

"How was the mall, Shoelace?" Wick says.

"His name's America," Fish goes.

Wick's sitting on the edge of his bed with his silver balls. There's two of them, and they fit into the palm of his hand. They have jingle things inside them. You're supposed to be able to rotate them around each other with your fingers all smooth so the jingle things don't ring. Wick can't do it. The jingle things are always dinging all over the place.

I watch myself ignore him while I hang my shoe-laces up on my hooks.

"Is that all he got?" Wick asks.

"That's it," Ernie says. "Except for some pizza. What's wrong with him?" He means Marshall. Marshall's lying on his bed with his face in his pillow.

"He's sad," Fish says.

"Shut up, Fish," Wick says.

"You shut up," I watch myself tell Wick.

"Yeah," Fish says. "You shut up." Then he pats my arm. Wick looks impressed.

"Marshall's mom was supposed to visit today," Ernie whispers to me. "I guess she didn't show. She practically never shows."

Marshall pulls his pillow out from under his face and throws it hard at Ernie. "Shut the hell up!" he yells. His face is so scrunched, those ovals above his eyes are straight lines again. He grabs his boot.

"Points," Tom warns, from the doorway.

"Fuck points!" Marshall yells, and he throws the boot at Ernie's face.

Ernie gets a bloody nose, and Marshall gets a time-out in the cool down room.

* * *

Mr. Patterson stops wondering after a few months. We play games, instead. Checkers. Monopoly. Connect Four. Uno. I look out over Mr. Patterson's shoulder into the field. Sometimes Mr. Patterson makes a note in his notebook. Sometimes he tries to talk to me.

Good game, he'll say. *Nice move.* He's so boring, I'll forget to move. There will be a long, long wait, and then he'll say, *You know it's your move, right?*

Then I'll move.

* * *

I won't answer to Shoelace.

"I'm talking to you!" Wick says.

"My name's America," I hear myself say.

"His name's America," Fish says. He picks up my hand. I watch myself let him keep hold of it.

"Show me how you do that," Wick says. He's pointing to my feet. My shoes are laced half sideways and half backward. "Show me."

So I show him.

At the dance he tells Shiri he thought it up. I see them kissing, and then Tom catches them and sends them back to their cottages. But before Wick gets out the gym door, Marshall shoves him, because Marshall was the one who was supposed to kiss Shiri. Then Marshall gets sent back to the cottage, too.

"They're so stupid," Ernie tells me. "Don't you think they're stupid?"

I watch myself not answer him while people dance. Fish is there, jumping up and down all by himself. There's no skates and there's no park. What's there is music and people smiling.

◆ ◆ ◆

Mr. Patterson leaves Applegate. I get another therapist. Her name is April.

"How do you feel about being in therapy?" April asks. There's a new picture on the wall, and the desk is in the corner now. The chair with the worn seat is under the window. There's nothing for me to look at but some new plant. It's as big as a person.

"Huh?" I say.

"What's it like being in therapy?" April asks. I watch myself shrug. "Mr. Patterson mentioned that you're not much of a talker." I shrug again. "That's fine," April says. "You don't have to talk if you don't feel like it." The plant is all green leaves. They're stiff and look like plastic. "What if I tell you a little about myself?" April says. Then she does.

She's a student, and she'll be leaving in June. She sees therapy as a journey that is to be taken together. Therapy is all about discovery. It can be painful and it can be joyful, but it is always useful. She will follow my lead.

◆ ◆ ◆

Fish and me don't play baseball. They try to get us to, but we won't.

"I don't want to," Fish says.

"Come on," Tom answers. "Both of you. We need two more."

"It's free time," Fish says. "Free time means I can do what I want. Right, America?"

"Right," I watch myself tell him.

"It'll be fun," Tom says.

"Hurry up!" Wick yells.

"Forget them," Marshall goes. "Let's play, already."

Fish and me sit behind the fence, behind home plate.

"Batter, batter, batter, batter," Fish says.

"Nobody's up, man," I see myself say. They're still flipping to see who bats first.

"I like it when the ball pops," Fish says, putting his head on my shoulder. He means he likes the sound when the bat hits the ball.

"Wipe your chin," I hear myself tell him.

❖ ❖ ❖

"Sometimes it's difficult to talk with someone you don't know yet, because it's difficult to know if you can trust them." April has three pairs of glasses. These have green rims around the eye part, and pink around the head and ear part. "And sometimes it's difficult to trust someone who is of a different ethnicity." I watch myself dig in my back pocket and pull out a black pair of laces and a white pair. I watch myself lean down and get a zebra going on my left foot. "For example," April says. "I'm white. And you're not." I finish my left foot and start on my right. "You're Hispanic. And so that makes us different." I see myself take out the old brown laces and tie them together. I watch myself make a loop out of them. "Difference makes it hard to trust, and lack of trust makes it hard to talk," April says. "Don't you think?"

I watch myself slide the old brown laces over my hands, keeping my wrists facing each other, like the girls do in class. The girls know how to make a ladder and a teacup with string and their fingers. I watch myself trying to figure out how they do it, but I can't.

• • •

Fish goes to the dances, but he never asks anyone to dance. He used to jump up and down all by himself, but now me and him lean against the wall and watch.

"Shiri is hot," Fish tells me. He doesn't know what it means. "You're hot, too," he tells me.

Shiri comes over. "Hey, Fish," she says. "Want to dance?" Then she cracks up.

"Nah," Fish says. "I don't want to."

"What about you, Shoelace?" Shiri says.

"His name's not Shoelace," Fish tells her. He pats my hand. "It's America."

• • •

They use tablecloths on Sundays. Fish and me and Ernie watch the visitors. Wick's grandfather brings his own salt and pepper shaker. Wick watches his points when his grandfather visits. Marshall sits with Wick and his grandfather on the Sundays his mother doesn't show up, which is a lot of Sundays. She wears big earrings and a lot of bracelets that clang and sound sort of like Wick's silver balls. Marshall gets quiet when his mother's around. Ernie's mom visits once. She brings him a care package of home-made chocolate-chip cookies, which Ernie throws out, and a bunch of candy bars, which he shares with the rest of us.

"Those cookies looked good, man," Marshall says.

"Yeah, but you know my mom," Ernie says.

"Does Shoelace know?" Marshall asks.

"No," Ernie says.

"His mom puts weird shit in her baking," Wick says. "Capers and Ex-Lax and shit."

"What's capers?" Fish says.

"They're salty," Ernie says.

"Your mom's a freak," Wick says.

"Yeah," Ernie says.

"She only visits when it's her visiting day," Marshall tells me. "If you know what I mean."

"Shoelace doesn't give a shit," Wick says. "He couldn't care less."

●　●　●

"So next week will be my last week," April says. She's been telling me that forever. "How do you feel about our work together?" I watch myself stare at the plastic-looking plant. Some of the leaves are off. They're lying on the floor, and now they're brown. "That's all right," April says. "You don't have to talk if you don't want to." She crosses her legs. "Maybe I'll share with you some of my feelings about our work together."

She tells me how much I've meant to her. She

tells me she's learned so much from me. She tells me the journey will continue even though she won't be here to participate anymore. She'll be here in spirit, she says, just not in body. She tells me that she appreciates my spending time with her so many afternoons. She tells me she'll miss me. She pulls out a tissue and wipes her eyes underneath her glasses. Round and gold colored.

• • •

Fish never had any visitors, but he's leaving. Tom has a party for him during evening free time. There's a cake. Tom asks me to light the candles. He hands me a Bic. I watch myself watching the flame. The blue and the orange. And the black line where they meet.

Wick gets loud. "Who's taking him?" he asks. He's kicking at his silver balls. They're dinging and clunking all over the floor. They're loud.

"You'll have to ask Fish that," Tom answers.

"Who's taking you, Fish Head?" Wick asks. He kicks those balls everywhere.

"Don't yell at him," I watch myself warn.

"Don't yell at me," Fish says.

"Watch it," Tom says to Wick.

"Who the fuck is taking you?" Wick goes.

"These people," Fish says. "I'm allowed."

"Somebody wanted him?" Wick goes to Tom. "Who wants a retard?"

"That's enough," Tom says.

Fish holds out a napkin with cake on it to Wick. Wick knocks Fish's hand away hard. Fish knocks

Wick in the head. "You're ruining my party!" he cries.

"Outside. Now," Tom says to Wick. They go outside. Fish keeps yelling, "He ruined my party!"

"Shut up, Fish," I watch myself tell him.

"He ruined my party," Fish goes, and he picks up my hand.

Then I'm not watching me anymore, but I'm in me, eating a piece of cake and tasting it and feeling Fish hold my hand and telling Fish okay but shut up.

I'm in me, and I don't want Fish to go, and it hurts.

—•—•—•—

"I hear you had some trouble this week," April tells me. She's wearing the glasses that look like somebody splattered different-color paint all over the frames. Red, yellow, purple, white. Ugly as sin.

"Whatever," I tell her.

"You didn't earn your usual points," April says. "You got into a fight."

"Whatever," I say.

"Maybe you're having some feelings about our work ending," she says.

"I don't give two shits about our work ending," I tell her. I pick up my chair, pull it across the room, and turn it to the window. Then I sit down hard.

"Seems like you're pretty mad," April says, from behind me. I look out at the field. "But we still have to say good-bye," April says.

"So. Good-bye," I tell her. "Now will you shut the fuck up?"

Now

"Brooklyn," I go.
"Meat or fish?" he goes.
"Brooklyn," I go.
"Meat or fish?" he goes.
"Brooklyn."
He dumps a piece of fish on my tray.

— • • —

B.'s not coming back. What kind of asshole comes back to a place like Ridgeway, anyway? I walk up and down the main hall during our session time, and I watch the trees out the windows, all looking like skeletons, and I'm real sick of it. I walk up and down and I'm real sick of what's in my head. I'm sick of that shit locked up, banging all over my insides trying to get out every damn minute. I'm real sick of looking at it in there, like some damn thing I'm supposed to let run my sorry ass ragged. I'm real sick of it, because it's too goddamn heavy, and it makes me tired.

Ping. Pong. He's not coming back. Fuck him, anyway.

—•—•—•—

I throw my pillow on the floor. I put my arms straight down my sides. I wake up and my shoulder hurts, but I don't give a shit. I stay like that and don't sleep the whole rest of the night.

—•—•—•—

He's all dark, like he's been in the sun somewhere. "I was beginning to think you weren't coming in today," he goes.

"I was busy."

"Hmm."

"Plus, I forgot."

"Hmm."

"I did, man. Don't 'hmm' me."

"Okay."

"What?"

"What 'what?'"

"Why are you looking at me like that?"

"How am I looking at you?"

"Ah, shit."

"Maybe what you're picking up on is my wondering what it was like for you to have a two-week break in our sessions."

"I didn't give a fuck."

"Sometimes a therapist's comings and goings bring up feelings for people."

"Well, I'm not people, man. I'm me."

"It's just something to think about."

"What have I told you about me and thinking, doc?"

— ◆ — ◆ — ◆ —

I look out the windows of this main hall and I think. Here's what I think. I want that shit out, and plus, he came back.

— ◆ — ◆ — ◆ —

I watch Brooklyn from the back of the line, and it's near to being like War. The longer I watch him, the more I float, the more lazy I get with those cracks, the more those flashes slide through. Those gray and black squares and the air shaft. Clark Poignant's voice and Liza's bubbles. Mrs. Harper's angels. And Browning's sweet-smelling cigarettes.

I want that shit out.

— ◆ — ◆ — ◆ —

I want it out.

— ◆ — ◆ — ◆ —

I stand in the hall and look out the big windows at the trees. All naked and scrawny. Not good for climbing. Not strong with thick leaves and fat branches you can swing up on and climb into and disappear. Not like that tree back at Applegate, in the middle of that field. No good for a hanging.

— ◆ — ◆ — ◆ —

"You haven't said a word to me in three sessions."
"So?"
"I'm interested in what's going on inside of you."
"So?"
"I can't help but wonder if my going away affected you somehow."

152

"So?"

"I can sit here with you in silence for as long as you need, America."

"So?"

"Being quiet is fine with me. I just wanted to check in for a minute, to see if us being quiet is okay with you."

"Yup."

* * *

Hide-and-seek and the smell of paint and Mrs. Harper's walker and washing out my mouth with soap and sensational celebrity weddings.

I want it out.

* * *

He left, but he came back.

I want it out.

* * *

Slim Jims and elevators and flash cards and the 7-Eleven and Home Shopping and baseball and reading at night.

* * *

It's hard to know how to begin. It's real hard.

"You know what a cool down room is?"

"Tell me."

"Some hut behind the cottages. At Applegate."

"Hmm."

"It's got this soft floor. Soft walls. No chairs. They lock you in there when you mess with people. One window. You can look out at some field."

"You spent time in that cool down room."

"There's this tree out there. Has a bird nest."

He's quiet. I'm quiet. I want this shit out.

"When I'm in there, I see these people. Fish and Ty and Brooklyn and Mrs. Harper and Liza. Mostly Mrs. Harper."

"Hmm."

"I hate the cool down room."

"You hate it a lot."

"Yeah."

It's hard to know how to keep going. But he came back.

"Tom was always warning me about not earning points. I was always saying, *fuck points*. Tom was always warning me about language. I was always saying, *fuck language*. I was always using their towels and their toothbrushes, and I'd fight Wick all the time, and then I was always back in the cool down room, watching that tree. The one with the nest. That was a big tree. Looked like you could climb it, easy. Hide away up there behind those leaves."

He's quiet. I'm quiet.

"You want to play War?" I go.

"Do you?"

"Nah," I go.

We're quiet.

"I had these dreams. Marshall was always going, *Wake up, wake up, man*. Tom would be there, make Ernie turn on the light. Ernie would be all worried. *You okay?* he'd always be asking. It would be me, in the park, watching the skaters. Mrs. Harper and Liza and Brooklyn and Ty. They'd all be skating and laughing. There'd be this music, and I was watching.

I was on fire. I was burning up on fire, watching them skate. Nobody saw me, even though I was screaming. That was the dream."

He's leaning forward on his elbows. Listening. Listening real close. It helps you keep going.

"There was this one therapist. Thought he was some shit. Had a ponytail. Had all these tennis balls all around the room. Tried to play catch with me over his desk. *Catch,* he'd say, and I'd have to catch the damn thing so it wouldn't hit me right in the face. I'd tell him, *Fuck you.* He wasn't allowed to send me to the cool down room unless I got physical. That's what Ernie told me. Ernie used to tell me everything. So I'd say, *Fuck you,* and Tennis Ball would say, *Who pissed you off? Somebody pissed you off, right? A while back. When you were a little kid?* And I wouldn't answer him, and he'd say, *Was it the old lady?* and I'd leave and go mess with somebody and get sent to the cool down and watch the tree."

"You hated the cool down room."

"Yup."

"You liked watching the tree."

"Yup."

We're quiet. He's still leaning forward. Looking at me. Seeing me.

"Ernie used to bug me under that tree. He'd just sit down, all the time asking, *What's going on?* He'd be all worried about how I wasn't getting any points. No tickets. He was always wanting me to get to go to dances and take the trips and shit. I'd tell him to step off or I'd pop him a good one. He never cared.

He'd ask me to do his shoes. He liked the backward braid I used to do. He'd bring me new shoelaces. He knew I liked fresh ones. I'd tell him, *Leave me alone after this time, or I'll mess you up good.* Then I'd do up his shoes real nice. He'd say, *Tennis Ball's going to kick you out if you don't start getting points. If you don't start getting points and staying out of cool down, he's going to send you away.* I'd smack him upside his head, but he'd always find me out there by that tree, anyway."

"He would come looking for you."

"Yeah."

"That meant something to you."

"Tennis Ball is such a dick. He says, *Maybe it was your uncle.* I break his phone and lamp and kick in his window, and then I get all his stupid tennis balls, every single goddamn one, and nail that shit right at his face, and they drag me off to cool down."

"He made you angry."

"He pisses me off, man."

"He really pisses you off."

"That's what I'm saying."

It's quiet. He's quiet. I'm quiet. I'm real tired. I get up out of my chair and lie down on the floor.

"America?" Dr. B. goes.

"Just going to sleep a minute," I tell him.

"All right."

then

"Get Shoelace to do it," Wick tells Marshall after lights out.

"My name is America, bitch," I tell Wick.

Marshall wants a brand. He wants an oval, like the tattoos over his eyebrows, only bigger. He wants one on each of his shoulders.

"Well, I'm not doing it," Wick goes. "I'm not doing anything to mess with my points, man. I'm getting tickets, and I'm going to Great Adventure, and I'm doing Shiri, so help me God, and I'm not missing that for your goddamn circles."

"Ovals," Ernie goes.

"Shut up," Wick and Marshall say.

"You have to use a lighter," Marshall tells me. "I'll buy you a gold one."

"You're asking me?" I ask him.

"Yeah, I'm asking you," Marshall says.

"Okay," I tell him.

We do it while everyone is at Great Adventure. We do it in the cool down room. I hate the cool down room.

Marshall brings a lighter, rubbing alcohol, and a paper clip. The lighter is gold, just like he said. It has 24K stamped on the bottom. I watch the flame while he gets the paper clip ready. He unbends it until it's just a straight wire, then he pushes it into the shape of an oval, with a little tailpiece sticking out, for the handle. He takes his shirt off. He tilts the rubbing alcohol onto a balled-up part of the shirt and rubs his left shoulder with it.

"You're crazy," I tell him.

"Look who's talking," he tells me. His eyes are shiny.

"What'd you take?" I go.

"I don't know," he says. "Wick got it for me at the mall." He smiles some dopey smile. "From that man in the tie store."

"You're stoned," I tell him.

"I know," he says. "It was just this little pill." He hands me the paper clip, and I take it by the handle. Then I hold the oval part in the flame, the way he's told me to. Marshall leans against the wall under the white window bars. I watch the flame. The yellow, and the blue. And the black line between.

"Do you think Wick and Shiri are doing it right now?" I ask Marshall.

"Probably," Marshall says.

I keep holding the paper clip in the flame. Marshall told me last night I had to do it for a long time, to get it good and sterilized. The oval is bigger than the flame, so I have to move the paper clip around a little, to get the whole thing heated.

"She's probably sucking him off," Marshall says. Something about that and the fire makes me sweat. It makes my dick move around in my pants. I want to touch it, but my hands are full. And then I get this feeling that I know, that I hate, that makes me want to be dead.

"Do it," Marshall says. He puts his shoulder in front of me. I hold the paper clip, still in the flame, near his skin.

"Here?" I go.

"A little higher," he says.

"Here?"

"Yeah."

I touch the paper clip to his skin, and it sinks fast. Smooth. Marshall screams, and I pull the paper clip out. It smells like shit all of a sudden. His skin, burned, smells like the nastiest shit, ever.

"Ah, ah, ah, ah," Marshall moans. He's crying. I put the paper clip back in the flame.

"You ready for the other one?" I go.

"No way." Marshall goes. "No fucking way."

I want to feel the paper clip sink in again. I want to smell that smell. It feels good, like something else I can't remember, and then it feels bad for feeling so good, and I hate myself.

Wick tells us all about it at dinner.

"She found a tour bus in the parking lot. Unlocked." He pours ketchup on the side of his plate. "A bench seat in the back. Cushions and shit. Girls love cushions, man. It relaxes them." He dips three fries into the ketchup pile and then shoves them into his mouth.

"She was into it?" Marshall asks. He already showed everyone his new oval. It's brown and red and smelly under his shirt.

"She couldn't get enough of it, man. She was so hot."

"How many times?" Marshall holds the edge of his sleeve off the brand. He tries to do it casual, so Tom and the other counselors won't notice. He says his shoulder hurts like a motherfucker when his shirt rubs.

"Three times," Wick says. "No. Four."

"Did you use a condom?" Ernie asks. Everybody looks at him.

Wick stops shoving fries into his mouth. "You're such a goddamn pussy," Wick says.

"Well, did you? She could get pregnant if you didn't. Then you'd be a father, and you'd have this baby, and you might have to marry her."

"He's unbelievable," Wick says to Marshall and me. "Un-fucking-believable."

"I'm just saying," Ernie says.

"How were her tits?" Marshall says.

"How do you think?" Wick says.

"Man," Marshall says.

"That's right," Wick says. "I'm getting a hard-on just thinking about them."

"Are you listening to this, Shoelace?" Marshall asks me. "Are you getting this, man?"

My dick is hard, only I'm not just seeing Shiri's tits. I'm seeing Wick's dick, too, and I hate myself.

* * *

BC7 gets a black kid. Some other kid calls him a nigger, and the black kid knocks out three of the first kid's teeth before they get him to the cool down room.

"Aren't you going to buddy up with your brother?" Marshall asks me.

"What?" I go.

"The black kid," Marshall says. He keeps his towel hung across his neck, dangling down over his shoulders, so if Tom walks by, he won't see the oval brand, which doesn't smell anymore but still looks raw. "Don't you people stick together?"

"You are so stupid," Ernie tells Marshall. "I can't believe how stupid you are. America's not black."

"Bullshit," Marshall says.

"The Muppet's right this time," Wick says. "Shoelace isn't black. He's Arab. You know. From camel land."

"No way," Marshall says. He looks at me. "I thought you were black."

"Retard," Wick says. "You're as dumb as Fish."

"You're the retards," Ernie tells them both. "First of all, his name is America. And second of all. He's Indian, not Arab."

They all look at me.

"Right, America?" Ernie says.

"Eat me," I tell him.

• • •

I hate lights out now because my dick has a mind of its own and my brain has a mind of its own. My dick gets hard and my brain thinks about tits and dicks, and I don't want to touch it, but then I do, anyway, and then I'm hotter than anything, burning up, and I hate myself and I wish I was dead.

"Finally," Wick says, before visiting hours.

"Finally what?" Marshall asks.

"Shoelace is finally choking his chicken," Wick says.

"His name's America," Ernie mutters.

"Whatever," Wick says.

"You saw him?" Marshall asks. His arm doesn't hurt anymore. The oval is black now. Not red. It looks pretty good. Marshall loves it. He's always pushing up his sleeve and checking it out when he thinks nobody's looking.

"Didn't see him," Wick goes. "Heard him."

"When?" Marshall goes.

"Last night," Wick goes. "Couldn't you hear his bed? Squeaks like a motherfucker."

"Was it good, Shoelace?" Wick asks me. "Did you mess up your sheets?"

"Shut up," I tell him.

"Shower's the best place," Marshall tells me. "More private. It all goes down the drain. No mess, no fuss. Right, Ernie?" He slaps Ernie on the back.

Ernie's face is pink as anything. "I don't do that," Ernie says. Wick and Marshall crack up.

"I don't," Ernie says. You can tell he's lying.

"Nothing to be ashamed of," Marshall says. "Only means you're a man. Right, Shoelace?"

"I told you to shut the fuck up," I tell him.

"Who do you picture, man?" Wick says. "Shiri?"

"We know she's off-limits, man," Marshall says to Wick. "Even for jerking off."

"You can't put limits on imagination," Ernie goes. Wick and Marshall smack him across the top of his head.

"So who are you giving it to?" Wick asks me. He leans in close and grabs his pants. "Who do you picture, man?"

Tits and dicks, you son-of-a-bitch motherfucker, I think. *I picture tits and dicks,* and then I hit him as hard as any goddamn thing I ever hit in my life.

* * *

I hate the cool down room. I hate the way you can hear people coming from a mile away, so you know you can touch yourself all you want without anybody walking in on you. I hate how it's so boring and quiet that when your dick has a mind of its own and your brain has a mind of its own, all you end up doing in there is grabbing yourself and thinking about tits and dicks until you're too tired to do it anymore and then all you picture is Mrs. Harper

163

turning her back on you, and you hate yourself and want to die.

• • •

I'm at the top of Mount Everest, and it's right where I'm supposed to be. I'm looking out at the clouds and the sky and the snow, and everything is white and icicles, and nothing is burning up or even warm. Everything is the way it's supposed to be, and I know my whole life was just a TV show I saw once and not even real, and I can't remember what it all was anymore, and then somebody is there, pulling at me with a string, or a rope, and it hurts, and I hear rumbling, and there's an avalanche coming right for me, and the rope hurts, and I'm smothered, and I can't breathe.

"America!" Tom's going. "America!" He's shaking me, and the lights are on, and Ernie and Wick and Marshall are sitting up in their beds, and they're real quiet for once, and Tom is shaking me and going, "America! America!"

• • •

The kid was nine, and he killed a man. He shot the man right in the chest. Then he threw the gun into a vacant lot and went to a baseball game with a friend and the friend's father, and he bought a hot dog, and he ate it, and then he won the class spelling bee the next day, and then he took the same friend to the place where the dead man was, and he showed the body to the friend, and he said he found it. Then the friend told his father, and the cops caught the kid.

Everybody's talking about it. Is he going to get tried as a kid or as an adult? Does a nine-year-old know what he's doing when he shoots a man? Is it the kid's fault, or is it the kid's parents' fault?

They make us talk about it in group. We have group now, until they hire another therapist. Tennis Ball left after I messed him up. What a pussy.

"What I want to know," Ernie says, "is why the kid shot the man in the first place."

"Would that affect how you'd think about it, then?" Tom asks.

"Not me," Marshall says. "Murder is murder, no matter how you slice it. You're not supposed to take another person's life. That's up to God."

"Since when are you such a Jesus freak?" Wick says.

"I'm not a Jesus freak," Marshall says. "You just shouldn't go around killing people."

"I'm going to kill somebody someday," Wick says. "I'm going to blow somebody away."

"Don't hang with me, then," Marshall says. "Because I don't hang with murderers."

"I'm just kidding, man," Wick goes. "Shit."

"Well, maybe you're kidding about the doing," Tom says. "But maybe not about the feeling."

"What's that supposed to mean?" Marshall says.

"It means," Tom says, "that it's okay to feel like killing someone sometimes. It's just not okay to actually do it."

"What if I feel like killing you?" Wick says.

"What if you do?" Tom says.

"What about Shoelace?" Marshall says.

"His name's America," Ernie says.

"What about him?" Wick says.

"Did you ever feel like killing somebody?" Marshall goes.

"Yeah," I tell him.

"So what did you do instead?" Tom asks.

"I didn't do anything instead," I tell them. They don't get it, except for maybe Ernie. He looks at me funny.

"What about the nine-year-old?" Tom asks me. "Would you want to know why he did it?"

"I don't care," I say.

"You must have an opinion," Tom says.

"I don't care," I tell him. Ernie's still looking at me funny.

"Shut the fuck up," I tell him.

"He didn't say anything," Marshall goes.

◆ ◆ ◆

I'm tired. I'm too tired to need the cool down room. I don't get points, though, because I'm too tired to get out of bed, and I miss class and chores a lot of the time. They send me to the doctor, but I'm not sick. I'm just tired.

"Get out of bed, Shoelace," Marshall says.

"Come on," Ernie says. "Get up."

"Move your ass," Wick goes.

I'm so tired, I almost don't even hear them. I'm too tired to hear anything. I'm too tired to eat, and

I'm too tired to dream. My dick is too tired and my brain is too tired.

"He doesn't even jerk off anymore," Wick says.

Tom sits at the side of my bed a lot. "If you don't get up, we're going to have to send you to a hospital," he tells me.

"So?" I say. But I drag myself up. I don't want a hospital. I just want to sleep.

Now

"Tired," I go.

"Yes."

"How come you don't care when I sleep in here?"

"I don't care?" Dr. B. goes.

"Nah."

"Maybe it's more that while I do care, I don't mind."

"Whatever."

"Do you feel like sleeping today?"

"In here?"

"Yes."

"Nah."

We're quiet.

"You want to hear how it happened?"

"How what happened?"

"I had this dream."

"A dream."

"I'm in the bathtub with my brother, and the water's green. He's trying to wake me up. He's all, *Yo, man. You going to drown in here.* I'm telling him, *Get off me,* and he's going, *What happened to you, anyway, man?* I'm all wet and cold, and I'm telling him, *We did okay, right?* and he goes, *You ought to come around more.* I tell him how I've been real tired lately, and he's all, *No shit. You almost asleep now. You best not drown in my tub, little brother.* Then I tell how I killed Browning. How I burned him up. My brother goes, *You hated that motherfucker, yo?* Then the bathtub gets deeper, and I start sinking. *Nah,* I'm going. *He was real kind.* I'm sinking fast. *Grab my hand,* I'm saying. *I can't swim.* My brother's all, *What?* looking at me like he can't tell I'm drowning. I'm yelling for him to grab my hand, but the water gets up my nose. Gets in my mouth."

Dr. B. is looking at me. He's looking at me with his elbows on the desk. He's real still.

"Then I wake up, and it's dark and way quiet except for Ernie. He's making some messed-up whistling sound, and I've got this hard-on and dicks are flashing through my head. Man hands and a man mouth and a man's body is all over my brain and on my dick and everywhere and I don't want to touch myself because I'm some goddamn motherfucking freak murderer and I'm so tired of that feeling good and that feeling bad like some kind of crazy trip Marshall had on some shit he got from the tie man and I just don't want it anymore and if you kill you should die because you're worse than

169

bad and you're bad, anyway, for liking it before it hurt and you take the shoelaces you've been collecting for fucking ever and you think they won't work but then you think they might because there's so damn many and you can braid them together and make you up a rope the way those dudes do it in prison, so I take the flashlight off the common shelf and I go quiet behind the cool down room to the tree in that field, and I climb it and work on the rope while the sun comes up, and I work on it fast and good, and figure out the slipknot and how to twist off this branch, and I'm thinking, *I'll never see Mrs. Harper again and Liza will hate me worse than she ever hated anything before, but who the fuck cares because I won't be around to care and that's the fucking point,* and then you want to cry like a mother-fucking baby, but you can't because you can't even breathe, and you think, *Real meaning is in the smaller things,* and then you're done."

Then

Ernie is yelling, and Marshall is crying, and Wick has my head in his lap under that tree.

"You stupid moron!" Ernie's hollering. "You stupid jerk moron!" When I look up at his face, I'm real surprised I've forgotten about his one brown eye and one blue.

"Shut the hell up, Ernie," Marshall keeps trying to say, only he's crying too hard.

My neck hurts and my throat hurts, and Wick, somewhere right over me is going, "It's going to be okay, man. It's going to be okay, America."

Now

Dr. B.'s there looking at me, and he's all quiet, and he stays quiet for a long time, and I stay quiet, and he stays more quiet, and we're real quiet. I think about hanging my head back to stare up at his ceiling or to check out those sand soldiers, but I don't, and it's still quiet, and then Dr. B. leans up out of his chair from over there behind his desk, and he reaches his hand out, and he's touching my shoulder, and I'm gone.

"America."

No.

"America."

No.

"America?"

It's high and clean and snow everywhere.

"America!"

No goddamn way.

"America!"

"What the fuck do you want, man!" I fall back down to standing on the other side of his office, and he's looking at me. "I'm sorry. I upset you, and you went up to Everest."

"Shut up."

"I did the wrong thing when I touched you, and I apolo—"

"I told you to shut up!" I go.

He shuts up, and leans back, and I'm still standing, and then he opens his goddamn mouth again. "I'm sorry, America, if I . . ."

I grab four soldiers off his stupid-ass shelf, and he ducks, and they hit the wall behind him and smash into bits. Good.

"Okay, America," he goes. "It's okay to be upset." I grab a whole handful more, and he keeps on, like it's nothing. "But I'm not going to let you distract us. I know this is difficult. Still, I think you can handle it. Drop those and tell me what just happened."

"I'll tell you what's going to happen," I tell him. "If you don't shut the fuck up."

"You're threatening me because you're afraid and angry, America," Dr. B. says. "I don't believe you want to hurt me."

I throw hard and straight, and they crash against his desk. He doesn't even jump.

"You don't know shit, man, because I've done it before, and I'll do it again!"

"What have you done before?" he goes.

"It's in the damn file," I tell him. "Don't you read your goddamn files?"

"I've read every word," he tells me.

"You haven't read shit," I tell him. "If you had, you wouldn't be talking to me so nice all the time. So motherfucking comfortable all the motherfucking time!"

"You don't like feeling comfortable because before, when you felt comfortable with somebody, that person hurt you."

"I'm going to mess you up."

"Sit down, America."

"Fuck you."

"I'm not going to be like that person, America."

"Fuck you straight up the ass."

Dr. B. looks at me, and he sees me, and he knows something, like he knows every damn thing, and I want to get back to Everest and I can't because he's looking at me. He's seeing me, and I can't go.

"I'm not going to be like him," Dr. B. says. "It might be difficult for you to trust that, but I'm not going to be like him."

"You don't know shit, motherfucker!"

"Put down your chair, and sit in it now," Dr. B. goes.

"Not shit!" I go.

"America," Dr. B. goes.

"I hate you," I go.

"Put the chair down."

"I fucking hate you."

"Yes."

"I'm going to mess you up good, now, motherfucker."

"Put the chair down and sit in it."

"Motherfucking goddamn son of a bitch." I go, and I make real sure to aim straight for his stupid-ass face.

• • •

It's not a cool down here. They call it a quiet room. It's all the same, though. They threw me in here after I did that shit to B. I slept some, and now I'm awake. I stay on the floor. If I stare long enough at the walls it can almost be like Everest. It's white and empty except for me. It's not for real Everest. I'm trying to get there, but I can't.

• • •

"They're talking about changing your meds," Dr. B. says. His cheek is purple, and he has a brown stitch over his eye.

"Don't touch me," I tell him.

He's in here, at the door. It's closed. The room stays white and empty. Except for him and me. "I'm not going to touch you," he says. "Can I sit down?"

"Don't touch me," I tell him.

He sits down. Right on his ass on the floor because there's no chairs. "They want me to change your meds."

"So?"

"They think you might behave violently again."

"So?"

"If I change your meds, it will be a lot different. You'll feel slow. You'll feel out of it."

"So?"

"I don't think you want to feel out of it."

"So?" He knows things. "Don't touch me, man."

"I'm not going to touch you," he says.

"Don't fuck with me," I tell him.

"I'm trying my best not to."

"You fuck with me, and I'll kill you."

"I believe you."

"I killed him."

"Your uncle."

"I burned his ass up."

"Yes. I believe you."

"People like me shouldn't be allowed."

"Hmm."

"Don't fuck with me, man."

"I'm trying not to."

"I want to work in the kitchen."

"The kitchen?"

"Don't fuck with me, I said."

"Why do you want to work in the kitchen?"

"My brother."

"Your brother?"

"Brooklyn."

"His name is Brooklyn?"

"He's got the white pants."

"J building white pants?"

"He works in the kitchen."

"I see. Your brother."

"Brooklyn."

"What's making you cry?"

"I'm not crying."

"Yes, you are."

"I'm not fucking crying."

"Yes, you are."

"Don't touch me."

"I'm not planning to."

"Don't."

"I won't. I'm just going to sit here for a while. Okay? Okay?"

"Uh-huh."

— •—•

They make him change my meds. I'm gone. I'm not here. I'm not at Everest. I'm not anywhere. Things are far away. I can't remember the thing I was thinking. I don't like it, but I keep forgetting that I don't like it.

— •—•

"How long ago was that?" I ask.

"Three weeks," Dr. B. says. His bruise is gone. His stitch is gone. Now there's just a Band-Aid. "You turned sixteen."

"Huh?"

"You had a birthday." He sits on the floor again. Leans his back up against the wall. Stretches his legs straight out.

"How do you know?"

"It's in your file."

"Fuck my file."

"I have a dilemma, America."

"Huh?"

"On the one hand, I don't want to ignore it, and I want to say happy birthday. But on the other hand, I'm not really sure what saying that would mean to you, especially right now."

177

"You've got too many goddamn hands, doc."

He stays quiet for a while, and he doesn't try to touch me. "How do you feel?"

"How do you think?"

"It's the meds."

"When is that shit out of my system?"

"Couple of more days."

"You going to put me in jail?"

"For what?"

"For messing your ass up with that chair."

"Actually, it was my face."

"What, you're a comedian now?"

"Hmm."

"You're not putting me in jail?"

"No."

"Why not?"

"It's not necessary."

"What are you going to do to me, then?"

"I don't know. What do you think we should do?"

"What 'we,' man?"

"We. You and me."

"Fuck we. I want to work in the kitchen."

"Oh."

"I'm a good cook."

"So you've said."

I'm quiet. He's quiet. We stay quiet. He pulls his feet up and crosses them, like he's young or something. Like he's planning on staying awhile.

"It was my uncle."

"Your uncle?"

"He's the one who taught me."

"Taught you what, America?"

"To cook."

"Oh."

"Browning. The one I killed."

"Okay."

"He was real cool at first."

He taught me how to read, and he bought me all those Tootsie Rolls and thought I was something, and needed me when he was lonely.

"He was cool."

He took care of Mrs. Harper and gave out dollars for home runs.

"He was real cool."

—— ● ● ●

I don't talk about it all that much, really. I tell it in pieces. Little bits about Mrs. Harper and Clark Poignant. Liza. Kyle and Lyle and Brooklyn. Browning. Sometimes we go weeks without me telling him shit. We just play Uno and War or stay quiet. Sometimes I flash up to Everest, but I do it fast and come back quick, so Dr. B. doesn't even know.

I don't tell him, either.

"I know this kid who used to jerk off all the time."

"Hmm."

"What, *hmm?* I just told you I know this kid who used to jerk off all the time."

"What reaction did you want me to have?"

"I don't know, man. Something besides that damn *hmm.*"

"People masturbate. It's natural. I'm not sure what you're getting at."

"Yeah, well. The way this kid did it, it wasn't anything natural."

"Is that right?"

"That's right, man."

"What was unnatural about it?"

"What he thought about, man. You wouldn't believe the shit he thought about."

"What was that?"

"Dicks. Dicks and tits. At the same time."

"Really."

"Pretty sick kid, right?"

"You seem to think so."

"He's a fag, right?"

"I don't know."

"What do you mean you don't know? He thought about dicks, man!"

"People think all kinds of things while they masturbate. It doesn't necessarily define their sexual identity."

"He's a fag, man. I'm telling you."

"What if he is?"

"Huh?"

"What if he is gay? What does that mean, exactly?"

"That shit is wrong."

"Being gay is wrong?"

"Faggots."

"Hmm."

"There you go again."

"You say this boy thought about girls, too?"

"Yup."

"Maybe this boy is confused about what arouses him. Maybe sometimes something about boys arouses him, and other times something about girls does."

"Can you stop with that *arouse* shit?" I go. "That word creeps me out, man."

"What would you prefer?" Dr. B. goes. He's so damn serious all the time.

"Whatever," I say. "Doesn't matter what word you use. This kid is still a freak, right?"

"Sometimes when kids have had sexual experiences while they were still very young, it affects what turns them on. And that's confusing and upsetting for them. Maybe if you ever talked to this kid again, you could let him know that you heard it's okay to have different kinds of things that turn him on. As long as nobody is engaging in sexual activity with a child or forcing sexual activity on anyone else and as long as nobody's getting hurt, it's okay. It's okay to think different things and it's okay to do different things."

"I'm never seeing that kid again, man. That kid is history."

●　●　●

I'm back on the regular meds. The stretched ovals. The yellow ones. Canary.

●　●　●

"Does Brooklyn get therapy?"

"Yes."

"You know him?"

"I didn't before you told me who he was."

"Who does he see?"

"He sees someone individually. And he has a lot of groups, like you have."

I don't even remember my groups. I used to watch that TV crack in the wall, and then I listened for awhile, and then I just started floating and that's what I still do. Stupid groups.

"What was he on?"

"I'm not at liberty to say."

"He was an alcoholic?"

"What do you think?"

"I hate that shit."

"What?"

"Alcohol."

"Hmm."

"Browning used to give it to me."

"Your uncle."

"He used to tell me it helped me relax."

"Did it?"

"It makes you all warm."

"How did you feel about that?"

"I liked it at first. Just like I liked the other stuff."

"He made you feel special."

"Whatever."

"You were a little boy, and all kids need to feel special, and he made you feel special."

"Whatever."

"It's okay for kids to like things that make them feel special."

"Time up?"

"It's not okay for adults to break the rules."

"I said, is time up?"

"You know it's not."

• • •

Dear Ernie,

I'm okay. I'm not going to do anything
stupid again. Tell everybody I say hey.
Tell everybody I say thanks for saving my
life and all that shit. Tell Marshall I say
he ought to get his other shoulder done.
Tell Wick Shiri was over here sucking

everybody off all over the place. Just
playing. I never killed anybody, Ernie.
That time when we were talking about
that kid in group, I know what I let
you think, and it's not true. I wanted to
kill somebody once, but I didn't do it.
Don't think I did it. Cool?

America

—•—•—•—

"Are you going to get Applegate to break that
age rule and take me back?"

"Do you want to go back there?"

"Whatever."

"What would you want?"

"Whatever."

"You feel like you want to get out of here."

"Nah."

"What would it be like to stay?"

"Boring."

"What would it be like to leave?"

"Whatever."

"Sometimes it's frightening for people to leave
after they've been here awhile."

"There you go again with that shit."

"What shit."

"That scary shit."

"Hmm."

"You're scared of your own shadow."

"Really?"

"Yup."

"What are you scared of?"

"Huh?"

"What are you scared of, America?"

◆ ◆ ◆

I watch them play. That damn ball is one pain in the ass when it goes off the table. Bouncing all over the place. Impossible to catch hold of. What am I scared of?

◆ ◆ ◆

"They hate me."

"Excuse me?"

"I'm scared they hate me."

I'm way up high.

"Who?"

I'm back.

"Brooklyn. Liza. Mrs. Harper."

"What would it mean, if they hated you?"

"Wouldn't mean shit. Would just feel like shit."

"What would make them hate you?"

"I'm a freak."

"Hmm."

"And a murderer."

"Hmm."

"I'm bad, man."

"Bad is complicated."

"You think I'm bad?"

"Do you think I think you're bad?"

"I knew you'd do that shit."

"Does it matter what I think?"

"Motherfucker."

"What does that mean?"

"It matters what you think, man. Stupid."

"Why does it matter?"

"You know why."

"Tell me."

"Step off."

"Tell me why it matters."

"Whatever."

"Okay, I'll guess."

"Huh."

"It matters because we have a relationship."

Up high and peaceful. Cold and white.

I'm back.

"And when we're attached to another person, we care how they feel about us. We care how they view us."

"So?"

"So. You did a bad thing when you killed your uncle. It was a bad thing, and there is no other way to see it."

"Told you."

"Let me finish."

"For what?"

"I don't think *you* are bad."

"That's playing. Doing a bad thing and being bad are the same. Everybody knows it."

"No."

"Yuh-huh."

"That's not what I believe."

"Well, you're stupid."

"Then I'm stupid."

"You are."

"Fine."

- - -

"Broccoli or cauliflower?"

"Meet me in the courtyard in front of C building."

"Broccoli or cauliflower, man?"

"By the fountain. Five o'clock, morning." He dumps broccoli on my plate. "Be there, Brooklyn. I want to talk to you."

- - -

Dear America,

Thanks for your letter. It was neat to hear from you, and I'm glad you're not going to do anything stupid again. Everyone says hi except for Wick. His grandfather took him right after you left. We have a new kid now. His name is Allen, but everybody calls him Tweezers because he's got one eyebrow all the way across his forehead. Do you know a girl named Liza? Tom said she called here looking for you. I know you're lying about what you let me think. You did it, right? I know everyone thinks I'm dumb, but I can tell you did it. Don't worry about it, though, because I know you're a good person. They would have put you in jail already if it was just because you're bad. I won't tell anybody, though, because it's probably

pretty personal. You should pray, maybe.
I'm not a Jesus freak, or anything, but I
think if you killed someone, it's probably
a good idea to pray. I told Tom I was
writing to you, and he says hi, and he
hopes you're feeling better. You are
feeling better, right?

Sincerely, your friend,
Ernie

•–•–•

"You believe in God?" I go.

"What do you think?" B. goes.

"What do you think I think?" I go back.

"Clever."

"Hmm," I go. I even raise my eyebrows. Just the
way he's always doing.

"Cleverer," he goes.

"Come on, man. Can't you just answer anything
straight."

"I've explained this before."

"So."

"Sometimes I want to answer you directly, but I
feel it's first more important to know what the meaning of my answers might be for you."

"It's just a question."

"Maybe."

"So you don't believe in God."

"I didn't say that."

"So you do."

"Do you?"

"I'm not saying until you say, B."

"What would it mean to you if I did?"

"If you did tell me or if you did believe?"

"Ah."

"Stop looking at me like that, man."

"Like what?"

Empty and sky and ice. Safe from anybody looking at me like that.

"America!"

No.

"America!"

No.

"America!"

"What!"

"I'm sorry."

"For what?"

"I scared you, and you went away."

"Nah, you didn't."

"I did, and I'm sorry."

"You didn't scare me, man."

"Hmm."

"You didn't."

"Uh-huh."

We get quiet after that.

"God," I say, after a while. "God can kiss my ass."

—•—•—•—

It's dark, and it's cold, and the fountain isn't even running, and he's here.

"What you want?" he goes. He's smoking a blunt.

"Where'd you get that?" I go.

"Why? You want some?"

"Thought you were getting clean over there in J building."

"I am. Haven't had a drink in four months, three days, twelve hours, and forty-two minutes."

"Oh."

"Yup."

"Didn't think you'd come."

"Whatever."

"So what happened? Whatever happened to you?"

"You tripping?" He says it, holding all that weed in. It makes his voice real little and stuck.

"Nah."

"What happened?" Now he lets it blow straight out.

"Whatever."

"You got me out here, five in the fucking A.M., so you could be all *what happened?*"

"Nah," I go, feeling stupid.

"Fuck."

"Where's Lyle?"

"The fuck should I know?" He pulls in on that blunt again.

"Forget it." It's awhile before anyone says anything. Then he goes, "We ain't shit."

"Huh?"

"We ain't shit. We ain't brothers. We ain't associates. We ain't shit. You got that?" He walks away with that blunt, and the fountain comes on real strong, real fast and unexpected, the water gushing up from all those little places, and Brooklyn jumps, and I laugh at his back, because why did he show up if we ain't shit?

* * *

"I think you're ready for the kitchen."

"For real?"

"For real."

"They're going to pay me?"

"Hardly."

"I'll still come by here?"

"It's by no means a full-time activity. You'll still come here."

"Huh."

"How do you feel about that?"

"How do you?"

"I'm proud of you."

"Well, all right. You answered."

"I'm full of surprises, America."

* * *

They were changing the whole system, anyway, and they thought I'd fit in real good to start. Now it's three different dinners every night. Three different cooking stations, three different menus, three different teams. They got two professionals running the show, with a head cook and three cooks under him. I'm the only kid from inside who gets to be a cook. At first, they show me how to work the stuff. How to use the stoves and the mixers and all that shit. How to cook for bunches of guys all at the same time. How to make big batches. I have to wear an old lady hair net like Brooklyn, and plastic gloves, and I have to keep count of shit. How many bags of potatoes we use up, how many tubs of beans, bags of rice, how many crates of fruit and vegetables come in and go out. I have to think and remember a lot of stuff. Have to check the burners and the ovens all the time when I'm done. Can't leave them on. Can't burn up anybody else.

"You got that obsessive-compulsive sickness, kid?" the head cook goes. "Godamighty. You check that oven more times than I got hairs on my ass."

"Nah," I tell him.

"What're you in here for, then? Shit, if you don't have that obsessive-compulsive thing, my apron ain't white."

"Depression," I tell him.

"You don't look depressed," he goes.

"I'm getting better," I tell him.

Then I check the oven again.

* * *

We're on a boat. In the middle of the ocean. Liza's hair is long again. She's hot, the way Wick and Marshall would think somebody's hot. Anybody would think so. She's smiling at me. She's saying, I don't hate you, America. Stupid. I don't hate you. The boat moves, and it's a whale. We're standing on a whale. She steps up real close to me and kisses my mouth. She presses up against me, and she has tits now, and they're soft. She lets me put my hands on them, and it feels good. She doesn't hate me, and she is soft and good.

192

My shorts are wet. There weren't any dicks. There was just Liza.

⸺ ● ● ● ⸺

I don't see Brooklyn in the kitchen, because I'm in the prep room, and he's in the serving passage. And he doesn't usually start until I'm done. But he's still here. I know because the head cook tells me. And plus, sometimes we end up not being shit at the fountain at five o'clock in the fucking A.M.

I ask them for sea salt and more garlic, and the guys start saying stuff tastes better. I ask them for gingered mustard, and I make them buy scallions.

"This kid's a real artist," the head cook says.

"Can I get some dried cranberries?" I go.

"Dried cranberries," he says. "Godamighty. Dried cranberries."

He gets them for me, and they go real nice in my gravy.

⸺ ● ● ● ⸺

We're on the whale, and Liza's hot, and nice and good, and then she lets me get in her pants, and she's got a dick, and at first it's cool, it's normal, and it's hot, and then real quick she turns into Browning and the whale starts diving under water, and I'm drowning, and then Browning turns back into Liza with a dick, and it's good again, and she hugs me real nice, the way a mother would, and it's all okay, and it doesn't matter.

193

———

My shorts are wet. It was Liza and a dick. Man. That is some weird shit.

———

It was good, but then they start finding the carrots. I've been getting rid of them every way I know how. Been throwing bunches out the window and through the grinder. Dumping armfuls down the garbage chute and the incinerator. I've been putting whole crates in the recycle bins and in the Dumpster in the back.

"You know who's been messing with the carrots?" the head cook goes.

"Nah," I tell him.

He comes back with a quarter crate. "I want half of these in the salad tonight, and I want the other half in the stir-fry."

"Yup," I tell him, and I wait for him to leave. He stays where he is. "The hell you doing?"

"Excuse you?"

"I said, what are you doing, man?"

"I'm watching you," he goes.

"Step off," I tell him.

"I want to see you handle carrots."

"You out of your tree?" I go.

"I get to go home at night, kid," he goes. "I'm not the one out of my tree."

"I don't like carrots," I tell him.

"That's what I figured."

———

"So what happened?"

"Didn't they tell you?"

"They said you were wasting enormous quantities of carrots. They said you were disposing of them. By the dozens. By the barrel."

"Yup."

"Must have taken up a lot of time."

"Yup."

"What is it with carrots?"

"Nothing."

"America."

"Dr. B."

"You liked the kitchen."

"Yup."

"You were good in there."

"Told you."

"You could be a chef one day."

"Yup."

"But what chef cooks without carrots?"

"I don't like carrots."

"Clearly." Then he starts smiling.

"What's so funny?"

"I'm sorry, America. I'm just imagining all those carrots."

"It's not funny, man."

"I know it's not. I just."

"Isn't that against the law, or something? Laughing at a patient?"

"America," he goes, all struggling to get his face under control.

"Shit," I go, trying to sound aggravated. "What are you, some kind of amateur? Now I have to deal with a goddamn amateur?"

I try to say it with a straight face, but that stupid laughing is catching.

— • • • —

I go out by the fountain at five o'clock in the fucking A.M., and he's there. Smoking a cigarette.

"Where's your blunt?" I ask him.

"Done with that shit," Brooklyn goes.

"Cool."

"The hell do you care?"

"Whatever."

"They say you killed a guy."

"Who says?"

"People."

"Huh."

"You did that?"

"What do you think?"

"What? You a shrink now?" It's something, how he knows about all that, too.

"You think I am?" I go.

"Man," he goes. "I hate that shit. That question-with-a-question shit."

"Yup," I go. He flicks me a cigarette.

"Yup."

— • • • —

I'm on the whale, and Browning's there, with a baseball, and we're throwing, and it's slippery on the whale's back, and we're throwing, and the ball turns into a dick, and it's safe, and it's good, and he's smiling,

196

and the dick gets bigger, and then it's not safe, but it's hot, but it's bad and not safe, but it's hot, and my dick is hard, and then he stops smiling, and the dick gets bigger, and then his face turns into Liza's, and she's smiling, and then it turns into Dr. B.'s, and he's not smiling, but he's safe, and the dick gets smaller, and my dick gets smaller, and then the face turns into Liza's, and she's got a dick, and it's hot, and I want to fuck her with the dick and all, and then she turns into Dr. B., and he's reading Ernie's letter, and he reads, I know you're a good person, *and then he turns into Liza without a dick, and it's not hot, and I don't want to fuck, and she's hugging me, and then we're not on the whale, but we're at Everest, and it's cold and clean and white and bright, and Liza and Dr. B. and Ernie and Brooklyn and Ty and Fish are all there and they're smiling, and it's safe, and it's good, and they're pointing at some shit, and it's Mrs. Harper in an ice wheelchair, and she's smiling, and she's going, America America.*

Dr. B. says every time I scrape a carrot or cut it or chop it, it can be me telling Browning how mad I am for him being real good to me and then turning it all ugly. Dr. B. says every time I scrape a carrot or cut it or chop it, it can be me telling God or Mrs. Harper or even Browning I'm real sorry I stole his life away like that. Dr. B. says every time I scrape a carrot or cut it or chop it, it can be me telling myself I'm done with all the bad, I am over all the bad, I am not all the bad. Dr. B. says I'll have so many carrots to do all that with that I can work through a whole lot of feelings by just cooking with the damn things. After a while I think maybe Dr. B. is right. So they take me back, and I scrape and cut and chop, and use up a lot of my head, going:

I hate you. Motherfucker, I hate you. Motherfucker. Motherfucker. I hate you. I. Hate. You.

And I take up some of my head going:

I'm sorry. I'm sorry. I am real, real sorry.

Little bits of a minute, I'm going:

I'm not all bad. I'm not so bad. I. Am. Not. Bad.

I don't know if this shit helps that much.

After a while, it doesn't even matter.

Seventeen Years Old

Brooklyn flicks his cigarette butt into the empty fountain. We watch the curl of its last smoke twist up and fade away.

"Won't be here tomorrow," Brooklyn goes.

"Huh." It's that time in the beginning of the day when the light is real little and kind of orange, and the birds are all twittery just like in cartoons.

"Going to get busted on a dirty urine. Going to get the twenty-eight-day special."

"Again?" I go. "You picked up again?" He got clean and picked up. Then he got clean and picked up again, and then he eloped. Then he came back, and he got a lot of months of clean time. Now it's all for nothing.

"Couple of beers. A blunt." He leans back on the edge of the fountain like it's his own front steps, or something. He's got the timing down perfect now, so he always gets up and out of the way right when the water starts running again.

"What happened?" I go.

"What up with that, yo? *What happened.*" I get used to the way he sounds like a smart-ass all the time. I don't take it real personal.

"You like the way it makes you feel?" I go.

"Nah."

"Why do you do it?" I sound like Ernie.

"Bored." He pulls a cigarette out from behind his ear and lights up again. He uses matches. He doesn't much like lighters.

"Dr. B. says underneath boredom is some other feeling."

"That dude got your head messed up."

"So why do you do it?"

"Make you get away from shit." He says it mumbled, the way you have to when you've got a fresh-lit smoke in your mouth, and you don't want it getting wet with your spit, and shit.

"Huh?"

"You high, you fly, you in the sky." That cigarette moves up and down the way they do.

He stands straight, real quick, and the fountain revs up with its water and noise like he pressed a button some way, only he didn't.

* * *

I prep the meat and prep the fish and scrape the cucumbers for ridges on the edges, and I think about it. You have to escape any way you know how. You have to get away sometimes if you don't get the life you needed. You can float up with your brain, or you can go find stupid Laura Ingalls, or smoke a blunt or drink beers, but somehow, you have to go far for a while. You get some peace that way. You get safe.

"You're kicking me out?"

"No. We're talking about an idea." Dr. B.'s sitting in his big back black chair with his feet up on his desk, all calm. All fine with it.

"You're kicking me out, man."

He slides his legs off the desk and leans forward on his elbows, the way he does that used to make me think he was paying real good attention. He's full of shit. Same as everybody.

"The idea of it makes you think you're getting left alone again."

"Fuck the idea of it. That's what it is, man. You're sending me away. Just when I started to like it here. Just when things were going okay. You're going to ruin it now."

You're ruining my party! Who said that? Fish. Fish said that.

"It's not meant to be a punishment, America," he goes.

"Fuck you," I tell him.

"Ridgeway has been anticipating the opening of this transitional living home for close to a year now, and I've been thinking it could be a good fit for you. Now that it's a reality, up and running, I thought it was time we discuss it."

"Ah, man."

"The fact is, there's no longer any reason to keep you here."

"Never signed your bullshit safety contract."

"You haven't needed to in a long time. In fact, America, you haven't needed residential treatment for a long time, either. Short- or long-term. The point is, now there are options."

"The point is bullshit," I tell him. I get up out of my chair. I start pacing. I'm big now. I'm big, and my steps take me all the way across his whole damn office, fast. I have to turn around and pace the other way. Back and forth. Back and forth. "You're not asking. You're telling. You're telling me I've got to leave. Probably need the damn bed. Probably have some other mental head tried to shoot himself or some shit, needs a place."

"What's this bringing up for you, America?" He's leaning back, and he's looking at me the way they look at you, and I'm pissed.

I grab his newspaper always lying there on his damn desk, and I start ripping it. I've got big hands now, and they rip real good.

"What's it bringing up?" he goes.

"Shit."

"It's bringing up shit?"

"That's right, man. Shit."

"You felt like you got sent away when you were small. When you ended up with your brothers. All of you alone."

"Shut up with that, man."

"You felt rejected and sent away and you lost Mrs. Harper. Things were never the same for you again. You thought all the bad things that happened were your fault. And that's what you're scared of right now."

I'm making these newspaper shreds mess things up all over the place. All over the floor, all over the air, everywhere. They flutter slow like ashes, and I think of that time when the ashes of my mother's chart floated all around Browning, when he was sleeping. Before he was dead. "Time's up," I go.

"You know it's not."

"Yeah?" I grab the doorknob. "It is for me."

Then I leave.

—•—•—•—

I cut and I scrape and I chop, and in my head, I go, *It's not bad. I am not all bad. I. Am. Not. Bad.*

You have to get away somehow. You can choose beers, or you can choose Everest, or you can choose the fountain at five o'clock in the fucking A.M. You have to find where it's going to be peaceful. You have to find where it's going to be safe. Maybe you don't get to stay too long and then you have to choose someplace else all over again. But you always have to choose.

—•—•—•—

Dear America,
Where are you?
Love, Liza
P. S. You better remember me

—•—•—•—

The fountain goes on at 5:17 A.M. I figured it out. You can set your watch by it, if you have one.

Brooklyn doesn't, so I don't get how he knew to stand up straight real quick all those times at the right second, but he knew. It makes a noise like a bunch of little bathtubs left running. I steal soap from the laundry, and I put some in, and now it's all white and foamy and crazy. I wish Brooklyn wasn't in detox. I bet he'd like it.

— • — • — •

> Liza,
> How the hell did you find me?
> America

— • — • — •

Sometimes from somewhere over my bed at night, I look down and I see me. I'm not that little kid anymore, I'm not all lazy and warm and bad. I'm this bigger kid, this almost-man type, and I've got big hands and a big face, and my feet hang off the end of the bed, and I'm not white, and I'm not black, and I'm not anything, but I'm a little bit of everything, and it's just like that. I look down and it's just me.

— • — • — •

> Dear America,
> Why didn't you sign, love, you jerk?
> Love, Liza

— • — • — •

"If I went, how would it be? And don't ask me how do I think it would be, or I swear I'll mess up this whole damn office."

Dr. B. leans back and crosses his arms over the top of his head, all relaxed and shit.

"Right now there are two young people living there. Another seventeen-year-old and an eighteen-year-old. There's a counselor who lives there, too. He's a social worker. His job is to run the house. To provide structure and support. There's room for a total of four young people. So others may join. You will attend school, regular hours. You would see me three times a week for continued sessions. Over time, you'd see me less often. You would maintain your medication until you, I, and the team all agree otherwise. You'd be allowed to work part-time if you maintain at least a C average in school. The money earned from any paid work would be yours to do with as you want. You would go to summer school so that you can graduate as close to eighteen years old as possible, or, if you think you can pass the GED at that time, you are allowed to try. You would be required to follow the general house rules including your share of chores."

He shuts up and looks at me real even. I don't even know what to think anymore. I don't know where I want to be. What I want to do. "Last week you said there were options," I say.

He nods. "We never ended our search for a foster family or foster group home, though the group homes continue to be over capacity, and families generally look for much younger children. Long-term treatment stopped being our first choice for you as of several months ago, though that's fairly moot, since there are still no openings in long-term, anyway. However, we could probably apply for independent minor status at this point, which, if you received it, would allow you to go anywhere and to do anything. It would also probably cut off public assistance payments for your relationship with us, here. You would still receive some assistance for rent subsidy, for food stamps, for medical care. You would receive much less for mental health care."

I know what it is. It's that I don't know where all I want to go because I don't want to go anywhere. Who could have figured that? Who would have bet I'd want to stay in some mental hospital? Want to be right in it, right where I am until—until I don't even know.

"Why can't I just stay here?"

"Why can't you?"

This shit. Man. This shit is hard.

◦ ◦ ◦

Brooklyn's getting fat.

"You're getting big, man," I tell him.

"Yup," he goes. He sits behind Dr. B.'s desk, in Dr. B.'s chair.

"Get out of there," I tell him.

"Huh?" he goes.

"That's Dr. B.'s," I go. "Get out."

"Shit," Brooklyn goes, but he gets out. His Dr. Rich is some ancient lady. I mean, she is real ancient. She sits down in my chair, and it takes her so long, the session's practically over before she's done.

"So," Dr. Rich goes, after everybody's all arranged somewhere. Her voice is like a tape played way too many times. All watery and thin and low quality. "We thought it important you boys have the opportunity to say good-bye for now."

"You leaving for real?" Brooklyn goes. He's not looking at me, though. He's checking out all those sand soldiers up on B.'s shelf.

"I told you, man," I tell Brooklyn. He's checking out the row of guys aiming rifles.

"Thought you was playing," he goes.

"No, it's the truth," Dr. B. says. "America is leaving. He'll be going to a transitional living home."

"Whatever," Brooklyn goes.

"The two of you can call and write," Dr. Rich says. "You won't lose track of each other again." That old voice. All worn out.

"Whatever," Brooklyn says. He stares at his knees.

"Is there anything you'd like to say, America?" Dr. Rich asks.

"Nah."

"Brooklyn?" she goes. He puts his head up and puts it back down again. He starts aggravating some scab on the back of his hand.

"I can't say it for you, Brooklyn," she tells him.

I look at Dr. B. He looks at me. He doesn't know what's up with this, either.

"Whatever," Brooklyn goes.

"You have something you want to say?" I ask him.

"Nah," he goes. But we all know he's lying.

It gets on my nerves. I think about it before I fall asleep, wondering what he had to say. Maybe he was going to tell me what happened to Lyle. Maybe he was going to say something about my mother. Maybe he was pissed at me for some shit. It gets on my nerves.

Dear Liza,
    I'm on a bus. I'm moving to a house at 101 28th Street in Park Hill. I've done a lot of shit. I guess you know some of it somehow, because you found out where I was at. Soon as I'm all in the new place, maybe we could hook up. I got you sometimes in my head, you know?
    America

We all have our own room. We share a bathroom, except for Phillip. He gets his own because he's the social worker. Ben and Kevin go to school. Kevin buses tables in a diner some nights. Ben watches TV and writes in his notebook. That's all he ever does. Phillip makes the weekly schedules and drives us where we need to go. Except Kevin rides his bike to work.

    "I'm getting a car, soon as I save enough money," he goes all the time.

    I don't even know how much a car costs. I don't know anything.

I wish I knew what Brooklyn wanted to say.

◆ ◆ ◆

"I'm not cleaning toilets," Kevin goes. "Can't function that."

"America? Ben?" Phillip goes. "How do you want to negotiate this?"

"He's cleaning toilets," Ben goes. "We're all cleaning toilets. We shift weeks. If he misses his week, me and America clean the toilets with his face."

◆ ◆ ◆

It's this different kind of school. Everybody in it's seen a lot of shit. It's like one big school for special ed. Only I know better now. It's not for if you're stupid and bad. It's more for if you've seen a lot of shit, and you did some bad things. Some of the younger ones, they don't know that yet. You can tell by the way they walk around. All big and in your face like they'd rather turn up dead than be some kind of pussy. They're real young, those ones.

◆ ◆ ◆

"We're running out of butter," Kevin goes.

I haven't cooked yet. They don't even know I can. Dr. B. says it's my choice to wait awhile if I want. I said I'd do the toilets if those guys would cook. I don't know why. Me and Dr. B. are trying to figure it out.

"Put it on the list," Ben goes. He's got corn bits all over his chin. He's always got something nasty going on. Too bad, because otherwise, he's all right. "Put it on the list, man."

"Can't function that," Kevin goes. "Somebody took the pen."

We look at the fridge where the magnet pad and the hanging pen are supposed to be hooked up, but the string is all wrinkled and empty at the bottom. It's just a little thing, but it gets me deep.

"What's your damage?" Kevin goes.

"Step off," I tell him.

· · ·

We need more than butter and a new pen, so Phillip takes us to a mall and gives us our allowance. I find myself a tobacco store, and I buy my ass a lighter. It's not gold, and it doesn't have any naked ladies on it. It's just red plastic. That's all it is. I find myself a shoe store, and I buy up all the laces they've got, which is fifty-seven pairs. I put the lighter and the laces in a plastic grocery bag under my bed. I don't tell anybody. Not even Dr. B.

· · ·

Dear Liza,
You can come by if you want.
America

· · ·

I still won't cook, but food makes me think about Mrs. Harper. She used those wooden toothpicks. She would just sit them in her mouth after a meal and work them around from one side to the other. She'd be there, maybe with some scarf all wrapped around her head, or maybe not, but with that little sliver jerking up and down and squirming its way across, like a cigarette, or some kind of pet.

210

I'm into his bookcase, checking out those armies. Thing is, once I get past the third row on all those shelves, turns out it's more than just soldiers. B.'s got everything. Little men and ladies and kids and houses and boats and furniture and baseball teams and farmhouses and cars and shit you didn't even know they could make out of sand. They go rows and rows back behind each other. He's got so many, I haven't even seen what all he's got.

"Liza's coming by the house sometime," I say.

I set up some of this new shit on his desk. I take these sand clowns and sand elephants and a sand ringmaster and a sand circus tent. I'm fixing up a scene.

"Is that right?"

"That's right, man."

"How do you feel about that?"

"How do you think?"

"You're in a playful mood today."

"Playful?" I go. I add a sand tiger and a sand motorcycle with a stuntman standing on the seat.

"Hmm."

"It's called a good mood, B.," I go. "I can be in a good mood, man."

"That's true."

"When's Brooklyn getting out?" I find a couple of sand clowns. I put them all around the tiger.

"What do you mean?"

"When's he through in J building? When's he done here?"

"I'm not sure how to answer that."

"He can move in with me and Ben and Kevin." That makes me laugh. Brooklyn would rip those dudes to pieces.

"Hmm." One of the sand clowns has a rubber hat. It comes off. It bounces pretty good.

"Just got to get him clean for a while, and then, boom. He's in." I bounce the rubber hat, and it lands right in Dr. B.'s coffee.

"What?" I go.

"I'm waiting for you to fish it out," he goes.

"Can't function that, man," I tell him. Then I check out the clock. "Time's up, B." I take off. "Later."

* * *

Dear Mrs. Harper,

They told me somebody can read this to you even though you can't read it yourself too good. I'm seventeen now, if you weren't real sure. I'm thinking maybe I could come see you. I'm thinking I could do that and tell you to your face I'm real sorry for all the trouble I caused you. I'm thinking a lot lately. Thought you might want to know.

America

That's what I imagine I could write.

* * *

I'm not even sitting down before he's talking, which is not cool right there, because I'm always the one who starts things off.

212

"America, I've got some news."

He's doing that leaning forward thing, that elbows-on-the-desk shit.

"What?" I go.

"Brooklyn eloped again, yesterday."

"Huh?" I go, even though I heard him fine. Sometimes you do that. You say stuff just to fill in when you don't want to do anything else.

"He ran away."

"I know what 'eloped' means, man." Sometimes I truly hate Dr. B.

"Dr. Rich contacted me last night, as soon as she heard. She thought you would want to know."

"Why the fuck would I care?"

He looks at me real long and hard, and he opens his mouth, and then he closes it, and then he goes ahead and says it: "That's pussy, and you know it, America."

Damn. You spend a whole life wanting real bad for someone to find you. But then when they do, you wish they would just leave your ass alone.

◆ ◆ ◆

It's a lot of people and a lot of buildings and no grass and no phones and a lot of green, and I'm walking up and down the halls, looking, and I'm looking and looking and looking, and I can't find him, and then there's an elevator, and Brooklyn's in the corner, smoking and crouched real low and smiling and going, What took you so long? I pop him on the head. Shut up, I go. You're it.

Then I wake up.

The TV breaks, and Ben is pissed. "Man," he goes. "What am I supposed to do now?" He's got nastiness coming out of his nose. It's always something with him.

"What about your journal, big guy," Kevin goes.

"Man," Ben goes.

"You could do some homework," Phillip calls, from the kitchen. "Wouldn't kill you, you know!"

"Thanks, Mom," Ben mutters.

The doorbell rings. I didn't even know we had a doorbell.

"You could get the door," Phillip yells.

Ben doesn't move. He's sitting sideways on this big armchair. He's got his legs all hanging over one of the arms. His fly is open. I'm never sitting on that chair again.

"Somebody get the door," Phillip goes. "I'm cooking us dinner, here!"

"Get the door, America," Kevin says. He's at the desk, checking out the porn on-line.

The bell rings again.

"Can't function that," I tell Kevin. Ben hoots. "You get the damn door," I tell Kevin.

"Or what?" he goes. He stops typing long enough to look at me.

"Or I'll mess you up," I go. He thought I was going to say I'd tell Phillip about the porn. I can tell because he starts closing out his windows.

"You will not mess me up, America," he goes. "Jesus."

214

I stand up from the couch real slow. It takes me a while to get all the way up, just like it took that Dr. Rich a while, only she was just old, and I'm big. I take my time and stare hard at Kevin.

He gets the door.

"America," he calls. "It's for you."

When I get there, he's grinning, and when he passes by me on the way back to porn, he grabs his dick. I'm so surprised to see her, I hardly even notice, and I don't even try to pop him.

"Are you people deaf or something?" Liza goes. "I rang, like, a million times."

<hr />

We walk around the block. It's a lot of wooden houses with porches and shutters and fences—the wood kind, not the metal kind—and trees with bunches of leaves and a smooth street you walk in the middle of because there's never any cars. She's not skinny anymore. She's real round. Her hair's long, and her face is all clear and red in the cheeks— not makeup red, but the natural type that comes out from inside all-white people when they're worked up, or some shit. She's not hot the way Wick and Marshall would think. She's not hot like Shiri. But she's real beautiful.

"You're huge," she tells me. "Look at your hands!" She grabs one and holds it up. "It's as big as my whole face!" Hers is round and warm, and her fingers grab my knuckles, and I get the water in my eyes. "You know what they say about guys with big hands, right?" she goes, and then she laughs, and we walk around and around and around until it gets dark, and we can hear Phillip yelling, "Ten minutes to curfew!"

— • • —

I thought she'd ask me what happened. I thought she'd say, *What did you do, anyway?* I thought she'd say, *You're a shit for leaving like that. Did you start that fire? You did, didn't you?* I thought she'd have her hands on her skinny hips, and she'd go, *You've got a lot of explaining to do, you asshole.*

But her hips aren't skinny, and she doesn't do any of that. She just tells me her mom says hey, and they found me because they always kept good track of Mrs. Harper and Mrs. Harper wasn't about to let me stay lost again, and sometimes Liza had these dreams where I was her father. That's all she says.

— • • —

Sometimes at night I wonder about all the people. Like, what happened to Lyle? Is he someplace with the Wheets, or is he dead, or what? Why did Brooklyn elope, anyway? He could be using somewhere on some street with people who beat you down for nothing. He could be anywhere, and I wish I knew what he had to say. And Ty. He was cool. He was real cool. Is he in some jail somewhere, or dealing on the inside, or what? And where's Marshall and Ernie and Shiri, and all them? Sometimes I get to thinking about Mrs. Harper, and I get to wondering, is she in some bed somewhere, all covered up with old-people blankets and watching Home

Shopping, or eating cottage cheese? And are they treating her good, and when she dies, is she going to be up there in Heaven looking down at me hard and then turning her back?

◆ ◆ ◆

Sometimes at night I pull out my red plastic lighter and my fifty-seven pairs of laces, and I look at them.

◆ ◆ ◆

We can't figure out the cooking thing.

"I just don't want to," I go. I've got a sand kitchen all set up with a fridge and an oven and a microwave and a dishwasher and these sand stools all lined up behind a sand kitchen counter.

"What would it be like to cook there?" Dr. B. goes.

"Boring," I go. He doesn't even touch that one. That shit is old, and we both know it. He just stares at me with his look. "Okay," I go. "We have the fire alarm the same place as it was at Mrs. Harper's."

"Where's that?" he goes.

"Over the doorway of the kitchen."

"And?"

"And what?"

"What's the fire alarm?"

I look for the sand one. "You're the expert," I go. "You tell me."

"I don't know."

"Well, neither do I."

"I wonder what made you think of it?"

"Me, too."

"Hmm."

"Hmm."

"Very funny, America."

— • • • —

I think about it. Something about cooking. Something about the fire alarm. I picture me waving a dishcloth at it, yelling how it's nothing, just something overcooked, or a dirty burner, or some shit. When I picture it, it's at Mrs. Harper's, though. It's not where I am now. When I picture it, Browning's somewhere in the house, just waiting for night, and Mrs. Harper's somewhere in the house, too, thinking how I always mess things up. When I picture it, there's the smell of things burning, and I remember the first naked lady lighter and the way his bed looked, on fire, when I walked out.

— • • • —

We have to sign up for spring chores. Cleaning the gutters. Fixing up the garden. Mowing the lawn. Trimming the hedges. I don't care, so Ben and Kevin pick, and I take what's left. Fixing up the garden. Phillip has to teach me. We use shovels and spiky ended poles to turn over all the dirt in the flower part and all the dirt in the vegetable part. Phillip says *dirt* should be called *soil*. He says *part* should be called *bed*. It's hard work. Your heart beats, and you sweat like a motherfucker. We work on the soil in the beds three days in a row before it's done. I'm sore in places I didn't know I had. I get black all in my fingernails. I don't mind it too bad. I like the way you can do that kind of work, and you can fly away while you do it without even trying. Phillip says he flies away, too. Digs and turns that soil for a whole part of a morning, and doesn't even know a second's gone by. Phillip says the same thing happens to plenty of people when they're driving a lot of hours at a time. It's just something people do.

• • •

Liza shows up before it gets dark on Sunday. Kevin grabs his crotch, and I pop him hard. He cries for real over that, and Phillip tells him he had it coming. Kevin says he's going to sue because there's supposed to be zero tolerance for violence. Phillip says the same goes for sexual harassment. Kevin says two wrongs don't make a right. Phillip ignores him.

"Are they always like that?" Liza goes.

"Yup," I go.

We're sitting on this hammock thing, strung out between two trees in our little backyard. Liza is real beautiful.

"My mom wants you to come over sometime." Liza's got a foot out over the edge, using the ground to swing us sideways.

"Okay," I go. "When?"

Liza looks over the beds. "Aren't there supposed to be flowers and stuff in there?" she goes. If you move just a little bit the wrong way, that hammock throws you all around like you're in the middle of the ocean. It's real hard to keep your balance.

"We're getting it ready," I tell her. "You've got to do a lot of other stuff before you plant." If you're not extra careful, the whole damn thing will flip over and dump your ass underneath.

"Oh," she goes. "You're getting ready for the shit part."

"The what?"

"The shit." She's wiggling all over the place, and I'm fighting just to keep my head above water.

"Huh?"

"You put shit in the soil. It's good for growing things."

"What?"

"Seriously," she goes. "They even sell it to people. In bags. I bet the next thing you do is spread shit all over everything."

I finally wiggle my own self real close to her. It's all uneven and bouncing around. I move real slow because this hammock is stressing me out, bad. "Stop talking about shit," I go.

"Why?" she goes. I kiss her for a while, and she kisses back. It's not a dream this time, and when I get my hands in her pants, there's no dick, either.

"Stop," she goes.

"What's the matter?" I go.

"I've been talking about it with my therapist," she goes. She sits up fast, and that hammock doesn't like it.

"Huh?"

"We've got something extra special, America,"

she tells me. Her eyes are real soft. She's real round and beautiful. "But sex isn't even the thing."

"Huh?"

"Don't be an idiot," she goes. "What we've got is bigger than sex."

"Huh?" I go again.

"God, America," she goes. Then she hugs me way tight, and I feel real happy and real sad right at the very same time.

He's there, all on his elbows, and I'm not ready for any more damn news.

"What?" I go.

"We received a letter for you." Dr. B. shoves some envelope across the desk. I check it out. AMERICA, it says, and it's got the address of the hospital.

"The hell?" I go.

"I don't know," Dr. B. says. He sits back. "But you're the only America we're aware of. So it must be for you."

I check it out again. The writing is all sloppy. The envelope's way wrinkled and kind of dirty. "I'm supposed to open it now?" I go.

"You can open it whenever you want," Dr. B. goes.

I flip it over in my hand. It's not from Liza, because that's not her handwriting, for one, and for two, it's not like she's got to write to find me anymore. It could be from anybody. It could be from Ernie or Marshall or Wick. It could even be from Ty. I guess it could be from Mrs. Harper, too. Maybe it's from her. Maybe that's why the writing is all raggedy. Because she's so old and shaky now.

Dear America, it maybe says. *Come and visit me anytime. I certainly do miss you. Mrs. Harper.*

"Who do you think it's from?" Dr. B. goes.

"I don't know, man," I say. "What am I, psychic?"

Or could be she wrote:

> *Dear America,*
> *Don't you dare come visit me. I'm done with you, and I don't need any more trouble. You behave now.*
> *Mrs. Harper*

"Who do you think?" Dr. B. asks.

"Who do you think?" I ask him back.

He puts his feet up on his desk and his hands on top of his head. The bottoms of his shoes are worn practically all the way through.

"What would be important about who I think it's from?" he goes.

"Ah, man," I tell him. He shrugs. Those messed-up shoes are getting to me. Maybe he doesn't get paid enough. If he did, he could afford a decent pair. That's what I'm thinking.

"America?" he goes, and then I forget about the shoes.

"Ah, man," I go again. I tear the damn letter open.

America,
There was some shit I been thinking
to say. It go like this. We shit. We
brothers.
Peace,
Brooklyn

I read it through a couple of times in my head, quiet, and then I read it loud to Dr. B. He slides his stupid shoes off the desk and leans in close to listen. My voice cracks on *peace*, but otherwise, I get it out okay.

* * *

Phillip lets me choose which vegetables. I plant corn, green peppers, two kinds of tomatoes, spinach, squash, and a couple of pumpkins.

"What about carrots?" Phillip asks.

"Fuck carrots," I tell him, so we fuck carrots. Phillip doesn't care. Now Ben and Kevin want a piece of the action. They see me out there all into it. They see me and Phillip figuring out when to Miracle-Gro and what to put where so the delicate plants don't get fried in the sunny parts and the rest don't get washed out in the muddy parts. They see how it's important work. They see how it takes some special thinking and a strong back and big hands.

"Step off," I tell them. "You had your chance. This garden is mine."

Liza's right about the shit. The actual shit. She's not all the way right, because it's not straight shit you spread out in the beds, but it's shit mixed in with other things. Nasty to think that when these vegetables come up, that's food coming up out of shit. But that's the way it is.

Phillip and them don't know it, but as soon as this garden gets going, I'm taking over the cooking. Me and Dr. B. decided I could do it. We decided not to let the damn fire alarm or anything else ruin something I can do good, something I can make a job from someday, something I like. We decided if I feel like going up to Everest when I'm cooking, well, who cares: I can just go. Or else, I can say inside my head: *Browning's not here. That's all history. This meal is for me and Kevin and Ben and Phillip. It's new, and it's not bad. There's no bad in this kitchen.* Dr. B. says that's called *positive self-talk,* and I say, if it works, I couldn't care less what all it's called.

— ● ●-● —

Sometimes at night, I wonder where Brooklyn was at when he wrote me that letter. I wonder what made the letter so raggedy. Was he drunk or high, or something, so his hand went weak? Or was he sick somewhere, real tired, and maybe scared? I used to think Brooklyn wasn't ever scared of anything, but I know better now. You can act real smart and big on the outside, like those little kids at my school,

225

but still be scared crazy on the inside. I wish me and Brooklyn had had a second to talk about real shit like that, because maybe if we did, he might not have run out, and maybe sometimes we'd still catch each other by that stupid fountain.

◆ ◆ ◆

Liza's helping me put these wire cages over the tomato plants and pull weeds. The knees of her jeans are wet and brown, and her hair's on top of her head somehow, looking like a flower up there, all spreading out in the sun. I'm real careful to knock her to the side where she can't smush any plants, but then I get her down under me, and she lets us for a while. I like the way she's so round and soft and tastes like a leaf. I like how she lets me touch her all everywhere.

"Get off," she goes, after a minute.

"Huh?" I go.

"Get off," she goes again, and the next thing I know, my ass is in the dirt. The soil. "I told you," she goes, pulling on her hair and fixing it back up again. "I don't think we should be fooling around."

"Why not?" I go. She is so pretty.

"Because we'll ruin things," she goes.

"Huh?" I go. Then I crawl up closer to her and pull her back down. She lets me kiss her again for a minute, and then she pulls away.

"Tell your doctor America says you're way confused," I tell her.

"I will not," she says. "My therapist is none of your goddamn business."

I kiss her again, and she lets me again. Then she pushes me away. My dick is going crazy.

"You don't even love me," she goes. Then she heads for the hammock. I hate that hammock.

"Huh?" I go, following her.

"You never even put *love* in your letters." She flops down so hard and quick, that hammock rocks before she's even set up in there. She doesn't make any space for me to get in, so I just stand over her, feeling foolish.

"Well," she goes. "Aren't you going to say anything?"

"What do you want me to say?" I go. I'm thinking I sound like Dr. B.

"I need to know if you love me, stupid," she goes. She sticks her foot out over the side and steps it to the ground to keep herself going back and forth. Back and forth. Ping. Pong.

Love. I don't know shit about that. It never came up with Dr. B. We never used that word. Never once. I think I'm not supposed to know what all she's talking about, but the real truth is, I do know. So I tell her, "Yeah."

"*Yeah* what!" she goes, all mad. I grab the side of the hammock with my big hands and make it stop so fast, she nearly falls right out.

"Yeah, I love you," I tell her.

◆ ◆ ◆

You don't think about it. About that word, *love.* Not if you're this not-black, not-white, not anything, little bit of everything, real big almost man.

It's way too pussy to even think about. But it gets on my nerves. Bad.

"You seem restless today," Dr. B. goes. I'm pulling sand statues off his shelves like a madman. I'm sick of those soldiers in the front rows. I'm sick of the circus behind them, and the hotel in the middle shelf, and the hockey team next to them, and the tennis players behind all that, and the ambulances and all this shit.

"Whatever," I go.

"Is something on your mind?"

I find some new rows behind the old ones. Rows I never saw before. Sand books and sand bookcases. Sand trees: a whole damn sand forest. "The hell is this?" I go.

"Buffalo," Dr. B. goes. "It's a herd of buffalo."

"Man," I go.

"What's on your mind, America?" Dr. B. goes.

Right when he says that, I see them. Way in the back of the bottom shelf. All different sizes and shapes. They're just sand color, and sand feel. They're not smooth or painted, or bright. They're with their chins in their hands, or sitting on their knees, or cross-legged, orfloating on their backs with their wings open or closed, or half flying. They're a whole army of angels. A whole damn army.

"America?" Dr. B. goes.

"You never told me you had these," I tell him.

"You sound angry," he goes.

"You should have told me," I tell him.

"I forgot about them," he goes.

228

"How could you forget about them?" I go.

"I don't know," he goes.

"Well, shit," I go. "Shit."

- • - •

Dear Mrs. Harper,

They told me somebody can read this
to you even though you can't read it
yourself too good. I'm eighteen now, if
you weren't real sure. I'm thinking maybe
I could come see you. I'm thinking I
could do that and tell you to your face
I'm real sorry for all the trouble I caused
you. I'm thinking a lot lately. Thought
you might want to know.

America

No.

Love, America

That's what I write.

- • - •

I get to noticing smaller things. The ladybugs in
the garden, for one. The way they seem like candy
for a minute, if you didn't know better. The way
Liza's hair is like red metal when the sun hits it,
slanted. The way the new dude in the house closes
his eyes when he talks to Kevin and Ben but keeps
them open when he talks to Phillip and me. The
way some teacher asks me to stick with this little
guy his first day at school. The way this little guy

keeps wiping his eyes with the back of his hand. The way this little guy says *fuck off* when I tell him I cried for damn near to a year once. The way he stands so close to me after that, I could step right on him and squash him to nothing.

— • • —

Dear America,

Mrs. Harper was glad to receive your letter and is eager to see you. She is not well enough to write to you, herself, but has asked that we make every effort to encourage a visit. Please contact us at the number on this letterhead at any time convenient for you so that we can arrange a reunion. Mrs. Harper sends her love.

Sincerely,

Riverside View

There it is again. That love shit. Damn.

— • • —

"What is it you want when you visit her?" Dr. B. says. I'm lining up those angels all on the edges of his desk.

"I don't know," I tell him.

"I think you do," he says. There's one sitting on its butt with its knees pulled up. The tip of its wing is busted.

"Just want to see her," I go. There's another one with its legs hanging from the knee so it's easy to set it on the edge of something. I put that one right in front of my face.

"What would it be like to see her again?" Dr. B. picks up one I put near his phone.

"Just want to see her," I go.

B. puts the angel back in the wrong place. "What would you say to her?"

I put it back in the right place, and he watches me. "I don't know."

"What would you want her to say to you?"

"I don't know."

"It may bring up a lot of feelings, America," he tells me.

"Yup." There's twenty-three of them.

"What's it like now, just imagining seeing her?"

"I don't know."

Their faces are the same, with the eyes all empty, but everything else is different. The way their arms and legs and wings are. All different.

"Let's take some time to explore this."

Sitting, standing, flying. "Yup."

"How does that sit with you?"

"Yup."

"Okay?"

"Okay."

* * *

Mrs. Harper sends her love.

* * *

This is one way it could go:

I heard you told them I went missing a lot of hours before he got burned.

Yes, I did.

Why did you do that?
Isn't that what happened?
No. I thought you knew I started that fire.
I knew no such thing.
I thought you did.
I see.
I killed him.
I see.
I'm real sorry.
You'll have to leave now.

⸺ • • • ⸺

Here's another way it could go:

I heard you told them I went missing a lot of hours before he got burned.
I did.
Why did you do that?
That's just what I had to do.
I'm real sorry.
I hope so.
I wouldn't ever do anything like that again.
Glad to hear it.
I missed you a real lot.
Good lord, boy. I missed you, too.

⸺ • • • ⸺

Or, it could go like this:

I heard you told them I went missing a lot of hours before he got burned.
No. I never said that. I always wondered why they didn't go after you.

232

I'm real sorry.

That was a sin, America. A very bad sin.

I know, Mrs. Harper. I'm real, real sorry.

That was my half-brother, you know. He took good care of me.

I know it, Mrs. Harper.

I can't understand how you could have done such a thing.

I'm real, real sorry.

I don't know if I can forgive you.

I know.

You'll have to work it out with God.

—•—•—•—

B. tells me to think about it and talk about it some more before I go ahead and do anything, but she could be dying right this second, and if I wait too long, it could be too late. Besides, it could go any which way, and by the time I think of every little thing, we'll all be dead. Dr. B. says it's good to process things before you do them. "Process" means talk about it to prepare, like practicing for some school report, or something. Well, screw that. You can process all you want, but there's nothing going to prepare you for the way this shit is really going down. I say, you just have to do it.

—•—•—•—

This official lady with a bald spot right at the top of her head looks real surprised to see me. "You're Mrs. Harper's son?" she goes.

"Yup," I go.

"Please sign in," she goes, and she shoves this

book at me. There's a space to write my name and a space to write the person I'm visiting and a space to put what time it is. There's this other space for me to sign what time it is when I leave.

"I was expecting someone a little older," the bald lady says after I'm done with all that writing.

Then she makes me follow her down this hall, and then down this other hall, and then down this elevator, and we land in some outside place. It's real clean with big flat circles of green grass and flower beds and benches set up looking at each other. There's all kinds of old people sitting in wheelchairs, and walking around real slow. There's nurses everywhere. Right in the middle of the whole place is the biggest circle of flat grass, the size of the whole downstairs of my house. It's all filled up with some statue of a fat man sitting on his fat ass, and circles of smooth rocks all around him, set up the way water ripples when you throw a stone in it. You wouldn't think it would be much to look at, a fat man and rocks and all, but it's real nice.

Mrs. Harper is in this wheelchair. She's got a blanket wrapped around her legs, and sure enough, a scarf over her head. She's all shriveled and dry look-ing, like the last part of a flower before it just breaks off and blows away.

"America is here to see you," the bald lady says. Mrs. Harper doesn't even move. "I'll leave you alone with her," the bald lady says, and she disappears,

234

and I end up standing next to Mrs. Harper, feeling foolish, just like with Liza and the hammock, only different, because I wasn't scared with Liza, only aggravated, and now my chest is thumping like a motherfucker right here. Mrs. Harper's staring over at that fat man in the middle of the rock circles, and I'm staring at her, and I see that ring, that black, round ring, hanging off a gold chain around her neck, and I feel like I could fall down extra easy, so I sit instead. I get my butt on the ground right next to her wheelchair, and I'm so big, my head is just about as high as her shoulders. I look at her awhile, and it's pretty hard to know if she can see or hear anything.

"Hi, Mrs. Harper," I go, and then I don't know what all to say. I scoot around so I'm more in front of her. So if she can see anything, maybe she can see me. "Been a long time," I say. She's real still. Sometimes she opens her mouth and then closes it right up again. We sit there a real long while, and I can't think of one more thing. Then I can. "Remember when we used to play hide-and-seek and shi—and stuff?" I go. She maybe looks at me a little out the sides of her eyes. "Yeah," I go. "Remember that?" The wind blows, and her blanket slips off her knee. I put it back. "I used to love that," I go. That word again. Love. You can be big and old and cool with being scared but nowhere near pussy, and that damn word can still get you right in the throat.

They let me wheel her to her room. An orderly goes with us to show me where it's at and then to lift her out of the wheelchair right into bed. When we walk in, I don't even bother to watch how he lifts her, to see how light she is, maybe. I don't even bother because of the angels. They're all the ones she did that morning. That first time I left. The ones with the reddish-brown skin and the greenish eyes with the fold down the outsides and the not-straight, not-curly hair. They're all the angels of me she did that day I remember, and when I quit staring at them long enough to look one last time at her, I know she's seeing me. I can tell the way her eyes stay steady right on mine, and by something about the way her mouth stays shut, and I look back at those angels, and I look back at her seeing me, and it's like I was buried under this avalanche all this time, for years and years and years and for-ever, and then somehow, some way, I just got dug right out.

◆ ◆ ◆

The official lady with the bald spot at the top of her head makes me sign that space in the book where it's what time I'm leaving.

"It's good you came when you did," she goes. "Mrs. Harper won't live much longer."

America, I sign. 3:43 P.M.

◆ ◆ ◆

I ask Dr. B. why Liza keeps changing her mind on me all the time.

"Why do you think?" Dr. B. goes, and I tell him he better learn some new tricks because his shit is getting old.

Me and Liza always end up fooling around after messing with the vegetable garden, and she always lets me get pretty far and then starts with all that bull about how it's going to mess us up if we keep on.

The peppers poke out first, and then the tomatoes, and me and Liza pick the ripe ones, and then I kick Kevin and Ben and the new dude out of the kitchen.

"Function this," I tell Kevin, when he starts to bitch about how I'm hyperaggressive, and I toss his ass out.

While Liza and me are washing everything, I get to noticing how tomatoes aren't truly red, like people say, but they're more orange with gold flecks.

"These are going to taste good," Liza goes. "Home-grown stuff is always the best."

"Can't believe it's shit made this garden grow," I tell her.

"Believe it," she tells me. "The more shit things get, the better they come out."

◆ ◆ ◆

Dear America,
We are saddened to inform you of the passing of your mother, Mrs. Sylvia Harper. We regret that we were unable to contact you prior to the memorial arrangements. Unfortunately, a

237

transition in staff resulted in the temporary misplacement of resident records, and so we were unable to find your information. Mrs. Harper died peacefully in her sleep several days following your visit. If you wish to know the location of her burial, please feel free to contact us.

Enclosed are your mother's personal effects, which, as indicated in her will, now belong to you.

We hope you will accept our most sincere sympathies.

Jessica Samuels

Riverside View

● ● ●

"What happened?" I sit in my chair and hand him their stupid-ass letter. He reads it, quiet, in his head. "America," he goes. "I'm so sorry."

"Whatever," I go, and then I'm crying like some kind of pussy. He doesn't say jack for a while, and I'm all trying to stare him down, all ready to curse his ass out for something, only he didn't do shit. "The hell is your problem?" I go, only it's real hard to talk when you're crying. He shakes his head, and he's got water in his eyes, and I can't even believe it. "You crying, B.?" I go. He shakes his head again. "You crying?" I go, still at it, my own self.

"What if I'm sad for you?" he goes, his voice all cracking.

"You try to hug me, or something, and I'll mess you up good," I go.

He shakes his head one last time, and then grabs a tissue from the box next to his phone and blows his nose. It honks like a motherfucker. "I'm not trying anything," he goes.

Grown

It's real late, and I know from the sounds of things that everybody's asleep, even Kevin is done sneaking porn and back, unbusted, in his room. I don't think about it too hard, but I haul my bag I got that day at the mall from under my bed, and I stay real quiet and take myself out by the hammock, next to the garden. After I look at the stars and the moon for a minute, I pull out the red plastic lighter and those fifty-seven pairs of shoelaces. I get the shoelaces together, and I tie them in one big-ass knot, and then I light them on fire, and I hold them by their own tail until the flame gets close to my fingers, and then I drop them right into the dirt. The soil. I watch until the flame gets almost used up, and then I stomp on it a couple of times, and then I throw my lighter so hard, I never even hear it land. Then I lie some more out here. And I wrap my big old fingers over the black, round ring hanging off the gold chain around my neck. And I think some things.

Like how when you're a kid, you don't know squat, and by the time you get older and figure out what you could have done and should have done and what everybody else could have done and should have done, it's too damn late. So you can have a lot of regrets if you're not careful. And how all that messed up my head so deep, it convinced me for a little bit of a while that maybe I should die before I hit eighteen, just to show for real how bad I was feeling. And now. Now I don't even know what all happened, but I'm thinking, *Damn. I'm here, I'm alive. What next?*

◆ ◆ ◆

Now, my big old feet stick way out over the end of the bed, and I can feel little bits of the garden stuck to my soles, and my skin's real dusty the way you get at the end of a day, and I'm thinking I ought to get my ass in the shower, but my eyes and my whole self is all heavy, so forget it. I'll wait until morning.

◆ ◆ ◆

We're angels. Me and Brooklyn and Ty and Liza and Lyle and Clark Poignant and Dr. B. and Fish and Wick and Marshall and Ernie and Tom, and we're all different. Some of us are the color of leaves, and some of us have blue edges around our wings, and some of us are silver, and we can fly. We can fly way high to get away if we want to but we don't want to. We're all over some big yard, and we're flying behind the weeds that

241

grow up at the bottom of the fence, and underneath the kitchen window boxes full of tulips and in the grass, and I hear, Ready or not here I come, and I hear, Peekaboo, and I hear, Where's America? and I hear, There he is, I see you, and then this big huge old hand from right out of the sky is lifting me up, gentle as all, and it's warm and softer than anything you ever knew in your whole damn life, and I am found. I am found.

A Word from E. R. Frank

As a clinical social worker who has practiced in Manhattan, Brooklyn, and New Jersey, I've known many Americas. They have been as young as nine and as old as fifty-six. Male and female. Unlike the boy America of my novel, most did not free-fall through the cracks of the system but became stuck instead: in prison, hospitals, addiction, homelessness, violence.

I've often wondered how useful a therapist's presence in the lives of these Americas could be. Usually their treatment is court- or school-mandated and seems limited, inconsistent. But what would happen if an America actually had the opportunity to be in one place at one time with one competent and caring therapist? Would it really make a difference? How could such a long-term treatment come about for someone not wealthy or grounded in a supportive family or community? Can a young person who has been traumatized several times over put himself back together again, and if so, how?

For me the answer lies in a healing relationship. It could be a teacher, a cousin, a neighbor. It doesn't have to be a therapist, but a therapist is whom I picked. Dr. B. was inspired by several supervisors and colleagues I've met and worked with over the years. He is effective, in part, not because he behaves perfectly, but because sometimes he makes mistakes and then handles his mistakes honestly.

But Dr. B. has a difficult task: America has experienced abandonment, sexual abuse, emotional violence, and all manner of loss. Not surprisingly then, America has been driven to the deepest caverns of his being. My belief is that a healthy, loving relationship very early in life, which is not tainted by betrayal, can be the mitigating factor, the one experience that can pull a person back from the edge of darkness. Which is why, in order for America to catch hold of Dr. B.'s lifeline, he had to have Mrs. Harper's first.

So America, Dr. B., Mrs. Harper, Browning, and all the rest in this novel are made up. They're complete fiction, except in spirit. That is to say, these characters are the result of my cumulative experiences and imaginings. They could easily have walked through my office door, but instead, they settled in my heart.

As many as one in three
Americans with HIV...
DO NOT KNOW IT.

More than half of those
who will get HIV this year...
ARE UNDER 25.

HIV is preventable.
You can help fight AIDS.
Get informed. Get the facts.

www.knowhivaids.org
1-866-344-KNOW